★ 3 BOOKS IN 1! ★

CLASSROOM 13

By **Honest Lee** & **Matthew J. Gilbert**
Art by **Joelle Dreidemy**

LITTLE, BROWN AND COMPANY
New York • Boston

Copyright © 2020 by Hachette Book Group
CLASSROOM 13 is a trademark of Hachette Book Group, Inc.
Cover and interior art by Joelle Dreidemy

Cover design by Christina Quintero and Elaine Lopez-Levine.
Cover copyright © 2020 by Hachette Book Group, Inc.

Little, Brown and Company
Hachette Book Group
1290 Avenue of the Americas, New York, NY 10104
Visit us at LBYR.com

The Unlucky Lottery Winners of Classroom 13
originally published in June 2017 by Little, Brown and Company

The Disastrous Magical Wishes of Classroom 13
originally published in September 2017 by Little, Brown and Company

The Fantastic and Terrible Fame of Classroom 13
originally published in December 2017 by Little, Brown and Company

First Bindup Edition: February 2020

Little, Brown and Company is a division of Hachette Book Group, Inc.
The Little, Brown name and logo are trademarks of Hachette Book Group, Inc.

The publisher is not responsible for websites (or their content)
that are not owned by the publisher.

ISBN: 978-0-316-42483-7

Printed in the United States of America

LSC-C

10 9 8 7 6 5 4 3 2 1

★ CONTENTS ★

★ **BOOK 1** ★
in the **Classroom 13 Series**

Unlucky
↓
THE LOTTERY WINNERS OF
CLASSROOM **13**

By **Honest Lee** & **Matthew J. Gilbert**
Art by **Joelle Dreidemy**

LITTLE, BROWN AND COMPANY
New York • Boston

CONTENTS

CHAPTER 1
Unlucky Ms. Linda

When *unlucky* schoolteacher Ms. Linda LaCrosse woke up Monday morning, she decided it would be another *unlucky* day. And she was right.

First, she put too much milk on her toast and too much butter in her coffee. Then she forgot her umbrella. It wasn't raining, but she used it to keep birds away. (For some reason, birds liked to swoop down at Ms. Linda and pull out her hair.)

On her way to work, Ms. Linda's car got a flat tire. No one would stop to help. She didn't have a spare tire, she'd left her phone at home, and it started to rain. When she walked to the nearest gas station to ask for help, the cashier was very rude. He snapped, "If you want to use my phone, you have to buy something."

Ms. Linda looked in her purse. All she had was a single dollar bill. "What can I buy for one dollar?"

The cashier pointed to three items. The first was a candy bar. The second was a pine-scented air freshener. And the third was a lottery ticket.

Ms. Linda had a mouth full of cavities, so she passed on the candy bar.

Ms. Linda was very allergic to pine, so she shook her head at the air freshener (after a very violent sneeze).

So Ms. Linda chose the lottery ticket. Being *unlucky*, she tossed it in her purse without a second thought. She would *not* win. She never won anything.

After Ms. Linda paid for the lottery ticket, the cashier let her use his phone to call a tow truck and a taxi.

When Ms. Linda finally got to her school, she was soaking wet and very late. The principal gave her the evil eye as she rushed down the hall in her heels—*click clack, click clack, click clack*—all the way to her classroom. Her classroom was number 13—which, if you don't know, is a very *un*lucky number.

"Oh, students, I apologize terribly for being terribly late," Ms. Linda said. "I've had quite the terribly—I mean, terri*ble*—morning!"

Of her twenty-seven students, twenty-six of them were present. Santiago Santos was at home with the sniffles. (The poor child was sick more often than not.)

Of the twenty-six students who were in class,

only twenty-four of them were awake. Of those twenty-four, seven were playing video games on their phones. Of the seventeen left, four were gossiping (which is not nice), and three were drawing pictures of butts (which is hilarious).

Of the ten students left, four were playing on the Internet, three were talking about TV shows, two were reading comic books, and one was picking her nose. (She could almost get the booger, but it was just out of reach.)

But of all twenty-seven students, *none* of them were happy that their teacher was here. They were hoping for an entire day of goofing off.

Well, except Olivia. Olivia raised her hand but spoke without waiting to be called on. "Can we start today's lesson already? I'm eager to learn." Olivia was very smart, but she was also very rude.

"Of course, of course!" Ms. Linda said. She pushed her glasses up on her nose and tried to straighten her damp hair (which was a mess because of the birds). "What shall we learn about today? Let's start with current events."

"My dad says the only important news in the world right now is the lottery," said Isabella. She had a horse on her shirt, a horse on her backpack, and a horse barrette in her hair. (Can you tell she liked horses?) "Right now, the lottery is worth *twenty-eight billion dollars!*"

"Oh my!" Ms. Linda said. She wrote 28,000,000,000 on the board. "That is a very big number indeed—after all, it has nine zeroes. Twenty-eight billion dollars is a lot of money. Who would like to do some math?"

"Boo!" some of the students shouted.

"*Ce cours est nul!*" shouted Hugo, who was from France and spoke only in French.

Ms. Linda remembered her lottery ticket and pulled it out of her purse. "Let's make it fun, then. This morning, I bought a lottery ticket. This lottery ticket cost one dollar. If I win two dollars, what percent is that?"

Only Olivia raised her hand.

"Do you think you'll win?" Ximena asked. "I hear the odds of winning the lottery are *less* likely than the odds of getting struck by lightning."

"I have heard the same thing," Ms. Linda said. "It is *much* more likely that I'll get struck by lightning than win the lottery. After all, I am very *un*lucky."

"If you win, can I have some of the money?" asked Fatima.

"Ooh, me too!" said Jayden Jason James (who other students called Triple J).

All the students wanted some of the lottery money. Ms. Linda shrugged. "I tell you what, class. If I *do* win—which is *very* unlikely—I promise to split my earnings evenly with every single one of you."

All the students in Classroom 13 shouted, *"Really?!"* (Except Hugo. He shouted, *"Sacrebleu!"*)

"Of course," Ms. Linda said. "I made a promise, and I must keep my word."

The students hopped up from their desks and huddled together in the middle of the class, whispering among themselves. Finally, they returned to their seats, and Ethan Earhart spoke up. "Ms. Linda? We value your word, but we would feel much more comfortable with your promise if we could get it in writing. Would you mind signing a contract and pinkie-swearing to share the money if you win?"

Ms. Linda thought creating a contract was a good lesson for the class. So together, they drew up a contract, which Ms. Linda and every student signed. Then, one by one, every student in Ms. Linda's class walked to the front of the room and did a pinkie swear with Ms. Linda. For the rest of the day, the students were nicer than usual. Perhaps Ms. Linda's luck was changing.

That day after school, as Ms. Linda walked home, she was struck by lightning—twice.

CHAPTER 2
Lucky Ms. Linda

When schoolteacher Ms. Linda LaCrosse woke up on Tuesday morning, she was in the hospital. She had survived both lightning strikes, and everyone kept saying, "You are *very* lucky!"

On Wednesday, when Ms. Linda LaCrosse woke up in her own home, she decided it would be a very *lucky* day for a change.

And she was right.

First, she put the right amount of milk into her coffee and the right amount of butter on her toast. Then she turned on her TV and saw the winning numbers for the lottery.

Ms. Linda LaCrosse had won.

When Ms. Linda received her winnings, she did exactly as she said she would and split the winnings with her students.

"Are you serious?!" asked Preeya.

"I am very serious," said Ms. Linda LaCrosse.

"But why don't you just take the money and run?!" asked Liam. "That's what *I* would do."

"Well, then it's a good thing that *I* won and you did not," said their teacher. She wore nice new clothes and had fancy laser eye surgery, so no more contacts. Her hair also looked very nice. Now that she had a limo and a chauffeur, the birds never had the chance to pester her.

"Are you really going to give us equal shares of the money?" asked William (who didn't trust anybody).

"Of course," said Ms. Linda. "A promise is a promise. What kind of teacher would I be if I didn't keep my word?"

In this lottery, Ms. Linda was the *only* winner—which meant she now had $28,000,000,000 in her bank account. "Twenty-eight billion dollars divided by one teacher and twenty-seven students equals one billion dollars each—"

"Hold on!" shouted Ethan. He held up the contract. "You only made a promise to the students who were *in* class that day! Santiago Santos was home sick."

"Yeah!" the students shouted.

"Wait, what?" said Santiago with a sniffle. (He was still sick.)

"But Santiago is part of our class," said Ms. Linda, "even if he was home sick that day." Ms. Linda wanted to be fair.

"Nope! No way! Nuh-uh," the other students disagreed.

"Think of the Constitution of the United States and the Declaration of Independence," said Ethan Earhart. He was a gifted speaker and a natural-born leader. "George Washington and Benjamin Franklin signed the Constitution. Santiago did not."

"That is true," Ms. Linda agreed.

"Thomas Jefferson and John Hancock signed the Declaration of Independence," Ethan continued. "Santiago did not."

"That is also true," Ms. Linda agreed again.

"And only the students who were *in* class that day *signed* this contract. Santiago was *not* and did *not*."

"That is also true," Ms. Linda was forced to agree.

"Then I present a question before the courts," Ethan said, as if talking to an invisible judge. "Would it be fair for Santiago Santos to take

money for a contract he did *not* sign? *We* have a right to that money, but *he* does not!"

All the students—except Santiago, who was wiping a rather runny nose—clapped and cheered.

Ultimately, Ms. Linda had to agree. "I am sorry, Santiago Santos. But you *were* sick that day. And we *did* sign a contract. I'm afraid you will *not* get an equal share of my lottery winnings."

For the next hour, Ms. Linda wrote a check to every student in her class—with one obvious (sniffling) exception.

Later that day, *twenty-five* students walked out of class with a check for over a billion dollars: $1,037,037,037.04 each, to be exact.

(You probably think I've made a mistake. But I haven't. Trust me. My name is Honest Lee.)

The next day, no one showed up to class except for Santiago Santos. He was still sick, but he vowed to never miss a day of school again.

CHAPTER 3
Mason

Mason was not the smartest kid in Classroom 13. He was not the most handsome (that honor went to Mark, of course). And he was not the funniest. But, man, could he play sports.

He was a natural-born athlete but loved soccer the most. He was the county's record holder for most goals in a single soccer game.

So, naturally, the first (and only) thing the

school's star soccer player bought with his $1,037,037,037.04 was a cow.

(Like I said, he was *not* the smartest kid in Classroom 13.)

Mason had been walking home from school with his check, when he met a farmer.

"Why the long face, son?" the farmer asked.

"Today I got a check for over a billion dollars, and I'm not sure what to spend it on."

"Well, that's easy," said the farmer, with sly eyes. "Buy a cow."

"A cow?" Mason asked.

"Of course! Cows are an investment. I have dozens of cows. Each one is worth millions. But this one right here? Daisy is special. She's worth well over a billion dollars. Heck, maybe even more! She's a friend for life. She can provide love and warmth all her days—not to mention all the milk you could drink! Add a little chocolate syrup, and *boom*! Ya got chocolate milk! Daisy here is priceless!"

Mason *did* like chocolate milk.

So he gave the farmer his check and took Daisy home.

Mason changed Daisy's name to Touchdown. That way, anytime he called for her, she reminded him of scoring a goal in soccer. (Which was incorrect, since a touchdown was a goal in football. Like I said, Mason? *Not* the smartest.)

But the sly farmer was right about one thing: They were instant friends.

Mason and Touchdown played soccer together (though Touchdown didn't kick the ball so much as just *moo*). They watched Netflix together (though Touchdown didn't watch so much as just *moo*). And they walked to school each morning (during which time Touchdown stopped to eat grass and would occasionally— you guessed it—just *moo*).

Touchdown provided Mason with fresh milk every morning, and Mason cleaned up the big piles of poop that Touchdown left in his front yard.

The pair were inseparable. The perfect team.

"I love you, Touchdown," Mason said.

"*Moooooo,*" Touchdown *moo*ed.

The soccer champ and the cow spent all day together, except at school. Even though they walked together, Ms. Linda wouldn't let Touchdown in the classroom. "Classroom 13 already has a class pet," Ms. Linda said. "Touchdown might make Earl the Hamster jealous. It's best that Touchdown wait outside."

Mason honored Ms. Linda's wishes. He left Touchdown to roam freely, nap under the playground slide, and graze on the soccer field all day. Before long, this turned into quite the problem.

Within a month, there was no more grass on the field—Touchdown had eaten it all. Instead of a soccer field, there was just a giant mud pit. To make matters worse, the other soccer players kept complaining that their cleats were covered in "cow pies." Mason didn't understand the uproar—pie was a good thing, wasn't it?

The school's athletic department demanded someone pay for the damages.

Not having any money left, Mason didn't know what to do. Luckily, Touchdown did. Touchdown took a day job as the school crossing guard. Nothing stops traffic quite like a cow in the middle of the road.

CHAPTER 4
Emma

When Emma Embry was a little girl, she begged her parents for one thing—a cat. She didn't care if it was a Manx cat with no tail or an alley cat with one eye, all she wanted was a cat. (She was so desperate, she would have been happy with one of those scary-looking *hairless* cats.)

But Mr. and Mrs. Embry were "interior decorators"—which is just a fancy way of saying "people who get paid to tell you what furniture to buy." And, yes, people paid Mr. and Mrs. Embry money (and lots of it) to tell them what kind of furniture to buy.

Because of their job, Mr. and Mrs. Embry were expected to have a perfect home. They had fancy furniture with long fancy names, like "Renaissance armoires" and "Louis XVI Baroque chairs." They had silk drapes and velvet carpet. Everything in their home was expensive or priceless or one of a kind.

That meant they would have absolutely *no* animals in the house that might pee or poo or vomit on their precious interior decorations. Thus, no cat for Emma.

Unfortunately for Mr. and Mrs. Embry, Emma came home one day with a check for $1,037,037,037.04. And she planned to spend every dime of it on what she'd always wanted: *cats*.

The next day, Emma bought every cat in the state—whether it was from a store or from an alley. She had them all shipped directly to her house. Within twenty-four hours, Mr. and Mrs. Embry's dream house became their *nightmare* house.

Curtains were shredded, couches were covered in hair, and anything that looked like a bird (or had a bird on it) was utterly destroyed.

"Our beautiful home!" Emma's parents cried. "What have you done, you terrible child?"

"For years, your home was more important to you than me," Emma said. "Now, my dream *pet* has ruined your dream *house*. Fair is fair."

Mr. and Mrs. Embry growled and screamed and threw a tantrum. When they were done, they told Emma, "If you have so much money, perhaps you and your cats should go live somewhere else."

"That's a fantastic idea!" Emma said. She'd always wanted to live on an island of cats.

Emma bought a large island in the Pacific Ocean off the coast of Polynesia. She renamed it Cats Island. (Not to be confused with Tashirojima, Japan—also known as Cat Island.)

Then she chartered a plane to take her and all her cats to their new home. She built a castle full of pillows and scratching posts. The televisions only played movies and shows about cats. Outside, there was a massive garden of catnip.

There was only one law on Cats Island:

NO DOGS ALLOWED.

Emma started a stray adoption service so that anytime a cat needed a home, it was flown (first class, of course) to Cats Island.

Emma finally had everything she ever dreamed of. There was only one problem—it turns out Emma is *severely allergic to cats*.

Her eyes swelled up, then sealed shut with icky-sticky eye goo. She broke out in hives, and

CHAPTER 5
William

All the students in Classroom 13 were careful not to use the p-word around William. You know the one—*paranoid*.

"I'm not paranoid!" William yelled. "It's not paranoia if someone's *really* after you. I'm telling you, we're all being watched. *That* woman has been watching me *all day*!"

"But, William," Ms. Linda said, "I'm your

teacher. I'm *supposed* to be watching you. That's how school works."

"Aha!" he shouted back. "So you admit you've been spying on me! It's a conspiracy!" He looked at the others with a smirk on his face. "Told you."

The other students were used to William being the most ~~paranoid~~ suspicious kid in Classroom 13. So, when William decided his life was in danger because of his lottery money, they shrugged it off.

"But, you guys," he said, "someone is going to try to rob me. Or worse! I just know it."

"Then hire bodyguards," Ethan told him. "Of course, if you don't pay them enough, they could turn on you, too."

William agreed. *Trust no one.*

He left school that day, taking a different path home than he normally did—in case he was being followed. He changed clothes as he snuck through the park, trying different disguises he had in his backpack: a neck brace, a nun's habit, a cowboy hat with a mustache. He finally decided to dress like an old man.

He folded up the lottery check and hid it in his shoe. He changed his outfit, stuffed his clothes with newspaper, then added an oversized scarf and a hat. "No one will recognize me now," he muttered.

Out of the corner of his eye, William thought he saw an unmarked car pursuing him with bad guys inside. He hopped on a bus going the opposite way from his house. It took him clear across town. *This will throw them off my trail,* he thought.

"You look just like my grandfather," said a young woman on the bus. "Please, take my seat." So William sat down. But then the woman started staring at him. He was sure that she wanted to steal his billion-dollar check too.

At the next stoplight, he ran off the bus.

When William got home, he ditched the disguise. But with each passing minute, he grew more worried. He was certain he would be robbed at any second.

He cut a hole in his mattress to stuff the check inside. But he became ~~paranoid~~ scared that the check would get stuck in the mattress springs and he'd have to rip it out. (Last he checked, the bank wouldn't accept paper shreds.)

He needed a new plan. But where would his check be safe?

William jumped when his bedroom door opened. It was his parents.

"Son?" his dad said. "Is everything okay?"

"Someone's trying to steal my money!"

"Don't be para—I mean, silly," his mom said. "Why would someone steal your allowance?"

"Not that money. *This* money." William showed them his lottery check.

"Oh!" his dad said.

"Why don't *we* hide it for you?" his mom said. "If someone is after you, no one will suspect we have it."

"And as adults, we know lots of great hiding spots," his dad added.

"Great idea!" William said. "Take that, bad guys!" He hugged his parents, thanked them, and went to sleep. (Being ~~paranoid~~ cautious all day was exhausting.)

The next morning, William peeked out his windows. No one was spying on him. His parents' plan had worked.

As he went to thank his parents, he found they weren't home. His parents' clothes were gone. So were their suitcases. And so was his pet goldfish, Goldie. "That's weird," he whispered.

William's mind started to wonder. Had his mom and dad stolen his money? Would they really run off without saying good-bye? Were

they thousands of miles away on a beach somewhere, sipping umbrella drinks and laughing about
their double cross? And was the goldfish—
that shifty-eyed sneak—secretly the mastermind
of the whole thing? And was Goldie even his
goldfish's real name?!

William chuckled to himself. *That all sounds
so...so...~~stupid~~ paranoid*, he thought.

Soon, William would learn that his paranoia
was correct. His parents *had* run off with his
money—and they were *not* coming home.

CHAPTER 6
Sophia

When she was born, Sophia was partially deaf. Now she wore hearing aids so she could hear. And every night, as she drifted off to sleep, she listened to "Sounds of the Rain Forest" on her laptop. (She found the exotic sounds of insects and birds and monkeys quite soothing.)

You see, Sophia loved nature. She talked to plants for hours, protected bugs, and hugged trees. (Sometimes they were rather long, *awkward* hugs.)

Because of that, Sophia believed the term "tree hugger" was invented for her. Per copyright law, she thought she deserved a nickel every time someone said it. Not that she needed any nickels. Now she was a billionaire.

After cashing her check for $1,037,037,037.04, she flew to South America and bought the Amazon. Not a piece of the Amazon—the *whole* Amazon rain forest.

Then she put up handmade signs all around it that read: NO SAWS ALLOWED!, PROTECTED AREA—KEEP OUT CONSTRUCTION JERKS!, and TREES ARE FOR HUGGING—NOT FOR CUTTING! (The signs were made on recycled paper, of course.)

She put up hundreds of these signs without using a single drop of bug spray to protect herself. After all, she believed that bug spray harmed the atmosphere and hurt innocent bugs.

But the Amazon insects didn't care about Sophia the way she cared about them. Sophia was bitten by twenty different species of bugs during her travels. By the time she was done, her skin was swollen with hives, warts, and awful rashes.

Next, she built protective sanctuaries for all the endangered species there. She paid local hunters to stay away and spread the word that the Amazon was "under new management."

"Whatever you say," the hunters said, shivering in their boots. Sophia's face was so monstrous from all the bug bites, she looked like a monster from a horror movie.

Sophia didn't care what she looked like. If the pygmy marmosets could talk, she knew they'd thank her. (Instead, most of them flung poop at her.)

Before she could buy Madagascar and save its rain forest, Sophia ran out of money. Property taxes, land deals, flights, bribes, and sign-making supplies were not cheap. The fat black markers alone were five bucks each.

Still, Sophia had saved the rain forest.

"I love nature, I love nature," Sophia repeated to herself over and over while she itched and itched and itched....

CHAPTER 7
Santiago

Santiago didn't get a dime from Ms. Linda's lottery winnings. That's what happens when you stay home sick.

CHAPTER 8
Ximena

Every day, on Ximena Xuxa's walk home from school, she stopped at the strip mall. She would high-five the florist, pick up some *caramelos* for her *abuela* (that's Spanish for "grandma"), and grab a new brochure at the travel agency.

(Her family couldn't afford to travel, but Ximena liked getting lost in the pictures of faraway islands and famous landmarks.)

But not today.

Today, with her check for $1,037,037,037.04, Ximena ran home as fast as she could. She skipped her usual stop at the strip mall.

The florist was ready to high-five her, but all he saw was a girl-shaped blur run by. His hand was raised but left high-five*less* in the air.

The owner of the sweets shop looked at her clock. She wondered if Ximena was sick. She always picked up *caramelos* for her *abuela*. But not today.

Even the travel agent—who let Ximena take all the travel brochures she wanted (free of charge)—was worried. The new Grand Canyon brochures weren't going to look at themselves.

At that moment, on the other side of the tracks, in the poor side of town, Ximena bolted through her front door like an Olympic runner.

"Mamá...Papá...Abuela..." Ximena said, out

of breath. She held up her check. "You're not going to believe this...."

And they didn't.

You see, the Xuxa family had very little money. Mr. and Mrs. Xuxa both worked two jobs and worked hard for every dollar. So they found it hard to believe their daughter could become an instant billionaire simply by showing up to school.

"You're right. I don't believe it!" Mr. Xuxa said. He stared at the check.

"Me neither!" her mom said. She kept counting the commas.

"Truly, *mija*?!" her *abuela* said from her bed. "I am so happy for you, *mija*. Now you can see the world, just like you've always wanted."

"Will you come with me, Abuela?" Ximena asked.

"I wish I could, but no. I am too old and too tired. But you should go."

Abuela was Ximena's best friend. She didn't want to see the world without her. But as Ximena stared at her collected travel brochures, she had an idea. If she couldn't take her *abuela* to see the world, then she would bring the world to her *abuela*.

First, Ximena *rented* the Statue of Liberty. She had it airlifted from Liberty Island right to her driveway. Ximena thought it was much *less* green in person than in the brochures. Ximena repainted the statue electric pink and gave her a pair of bright yellow sunglasses. (When she was returned to New York City, everyone seemed to like the new look.)

Ximena then rented Mount Rushmore. It was airlifted from South Dakota to her backyard. She agreed with the brochure that the monument was "impressive," but she thought it needed something extra. So she hired a sculptor to chisel her *abuela*'s face next to President Lincoln's. It was her *abuela*'s idea to add a mustache and a Mohawk.

Ximena called the French government about renting the Eiffel Tower, but someone had already bought it. (Ximena wondered if it was someone in her class.)

Ximena spent her fortune renting other famous landmarks. She rented the Great Sphinx from Egypt, the Great Wall of China from China, the Taj Mahal from India, and the Leaning Tower of Pisa from Italy. She even rented Big Ben from England. (Though it was only temporary, the queen was *not* pleased about it.)

Abuela loved everything that Ximena brought home for her to see—except for Stonehenge, which Abuela called "just a bunch of rocks."

When she ran out of enough money to rent new landmarks, Ximena had just enough left over to buy her *abuela* a brand-new (and very comfy) bed and a lifetime supply of *caramelos*.

Together, they looked at new travel brochures. They didn't have a lot of money, but they had a lot of love—which, like the brochures, was free of charge.

CHAPTER 9
Jayden Jason

Jayden Jason James (or Triple J, as some called him) was the most popular kid in the entire school. He had a standing invitation to sit at any table in the cafeteria. He was voted class president four times in a row (in the same election). And he was always the first to be asked to study groups, sleepovers, and birthday parties.

He was the closest thing to a celebrity Classroom 13 had.

But he never let fame go to his head. Triple J was a people pleaser and a genuinely nice person. If he missed someone's event, he felt terrible.

And since he was always asked to attend everything (and there was only *one* of him to go around), Triple J was exhausted all the time. He needed a break.

So with his lottery winnings, he decided to *clone* himself.

He held a press conference about it on the playground. Ava acted as his press secretary and pointed to kids in the crowd (one at a time) to ask questions.

"How many clones will there be?" Teo asked.

"With the new clones, there'll be enough of me to go around," Triple J said. "In the past, I know I've disappointed some of you because my schedule was overbooked. Soon that will be a thing of the past. I hate missing events!"

Hands shot up again. Ava pointed to Dev, who asked, "What do we call your clones? Will they have different names? And if so, can I name one?"

"No different names," Triple J said. "That's too confusing. We're numbering them. I'll be J-1, and the first clone will be J-2, and then J-3, and so on."

"We have time for one more question," Ava said.

Chloe shouted, "Cloning is *not* ethically or morally sound!"

"That's not a question," Ava said. "Looks like that's all the time we have for today. No further questions, thank you."

Triple J hired the world's most brilliant scientists to clone him.

"That is immoral!" one scientist said.

"It's dangerous!" said another.

"How will you know who you are?!" said a third.

Triple J handed them his money. The scientists suddenly changed their minds and got to work.

The procedure was a success. Within days, there were four brand-new perfect clones of Triple J. (You might think four isn't very many, but clones are quite expensive. You could buy a space station for far less money.)

Triple J put a plan together: J-2 would attend all academic events like study sessions, quiz bowls, mathlete meetings, and school play try-outs. J-3 would handle all the athletic stuff like baseball, basketball, soccer, and (of course) bob-sledding. J-4 would take care of all family respon-sibilities like birthdays, Sunday dinners, and movie nights. And J-5 (the fourth and final clone) would appear at all social gatherings like sleepovers, pizza parties, and recess.

Triple J would never miss a single thing again. (At least that was the plan.)

For one perfect week, the Triple J clones were everywhere at once. J-5 attended game nights at Fatima's while J-3 was bobsledding with Mason. At the same time, J-2 was studying with Sophia and Teo for their history test, just as J-4 was settling in to watch movies with his family for movie night.

Of course, the original Triple J (J-1) wasn't at any of these events. People began to complain. They didn't want a clone. They wanted the famous original Jayden Jason James. They wanted the real deal. Triple J was frustrated, but he wanted everyone to be happy.

Triple J decided to go back to the way things were before. He would be tired, but at least everyone would be happy.

Triple J held a press conference about it on

the playground. Teo acted as his press secretary and pointed to kids in the crowd (one at a time) to ask questions.

"Why are you giving up on your clone plan?" Ava asked.

"I want everyone to be happy," Triple J said.

Hands shot up again. Teo pointed to Dev, who asked, "What happened to your clones?"

"I sent them to live on a farm," Triple J said. "But instead, they ran away and joined the circus. Don't worry. They are all very happy."

"We have time for one more question," Teo said.

Chloe shouted, "*I told you*—cloning is *not* ethically or morally sound!"

"That's not a question," Teo said. "Looks like that's all the time we have for today. No further questions, thank you."

After that, the original, famous Triple J was back. Everyone was happy to have the *real* Triple J—not some secondhand clone.

Then again, how would they know the difference? Clones are the exact same in every way. They look the same, they talk the same, they even fart the same.

What if the *real* Triple J was the one that ran away to the circus?

Strangely enough, some of the students of Classroom 13 have wondered the exact same thing. I've told them just to ask Triple J the next time they see him...

On the basketball court...

Or at the spelling bee...

Or in the kitchen making popcorn for family movie night...

Or at the mall with friends...

Or...

Hey! Wait a second!

CHAPTER 10
Lily

Lily is a girl of few words. For instance, if you asked her how her weekend was, she would likely grunt, "Fine." Or, "Cool." Or, "Meh."

And if you asked her what she wanted to be when she grew up, she'd answer, "Astronaut." She wanted to go into space and explore the stars.

According to her dad, her first spoken word

was "NASA." He thought it was rather cute—because he thought baby Lily was mispronouncing "Dada." But no, she really *was* saying "NASA."

When Ms. Linda informed the class they were going to become billionaires, the other students talked a mile a minute about stuff they were going to purchase or things they were going to do. Lily only looked at her check and said, "NASA."

So Lily bought NASA. Yes, the National Aeronautics and Space Administration is now owned by Lily Lin from Classroom 13.

Lily's been tight-lipped (no surprise there) about the new rocket she has them building for her. I've heard construction will be finished in about twenty years. But if you ask Lily when it'll be ready for blastoff, she just says, "Soon."

CHAPTER 11
Jacob

Jacob Jones knew exactly what he was going to buy with his winnings. (Or more accurately, *who* he was going to buy.) He announced, "I'm going to buy a family!"

This confused the other students of Classroom 13.

"But you already have one of those," Benji said.

It was true. Jacob *did* have a family—but he didn't like them. He had a mother and a father who both kept to themselves. They never hugged Jacob, or spent time with him, or asked how his day was. Instead, when they came home from work, Mr. and Mrs. Jones would retire to their separate bedrooms.

To keep him company, Jacob left the TV on twenty-four hours a day.

There were lots of shows he liked, but there was one show he *loved*. It was called *Just the Twenty-Two of Us*. It was a classic comedy about the Jordans—a quirky family of twenty-two people crammed together in the same small house. If that wasn't hilarious enough, Mr. Jordan, the dad, was a basketball coach who treated his family like a team. When things got too crazy at home, he'd blow his whistle and shout, "Time-out! Family foul!"

Then everyone would laugh—the family, the

live studio audience, and, of course, Jacob. Jacob loved the catchphrases. *"Time-out!"* he'd repeat, blowing an imaginary whistle. *"Family foul!"*

(Jacob liked to pretend the studio audience was laughing at his jokes, too.)

Jacob loved Coach Jordan's family more than anything. They were always there for one another. And they were always there for him. He wanted to be one of the Jordans. But that wasn't going to happen. That would take a miracle...

...or $1,037,037,037.04 in cash.

The minute the check cleared, Jacob kicked his parents out of the house and moved all the Jordans in.

"Good-bye, Jacob Jones!" he said to himself. "Hello, Jacob *JORDAN!*"

Jacob was so excited, he greeted his new

family at the door by singing the *Just the Twenty-Two of Us* theme song:

> *"Having a family's like having a team,*
> *Twenty-two people LIVING THE DREAM!*
> *Our family's got game,*
> *Our family's got trust,*
> *So let's work together,*
> *Just the twenty-two of us!"*

When he finished the song, Jacob bowed. He expected his new family would cheer and clap and surround him with a group hug—just like they did on the show.

But they didn't.

In fact, not one member of the cast looked happy. Instead, Jacob's new sitcom family began asking him some very *un*-sitcom questions.

"Is this *not* catered?" Jeremy Jordan (the youngest family member) asked.

"How long is this gonna take? I have a photo

shoot at nine and another thing at ten," Jess Jordan (the older sister) said.

"What's the Wi-Fi password here? I need to watch my horse races," Jordan Senior (the grandpa) said, blowing cigar smoke everywhere.

"What's my motivation for this scene?" Coach Jordan asked Jacob. "Am I like, '*Family foul*,' or am I more like, '*Family FOULLLLLL*'?!"

Over the next few days, things got worse. His new family didn't want to sing their theme song. (Instead they complained a lot.) They didn't want to get into hilarious situations at the grocery store. (They didn't want to clean up after themselves either.) They didn't want to laugh over a family recipe gone wrong. (But they did expect five-star chefs to prepare all their meals.) They didn't even care if Jacob applauded when they entered a room. (In fact, they gave him strange looks when he did.)

Jacob didn't understand why everyone was

acting so weird. They weren't acting like the TV characters he loved. They were acting like...like... *actors*.

Hoping they would come around, Jacob gave them *more* money to act like his favorite characters. But they moaned and groaned the whole time. At the end of each day, their agents called and asked for more money.

And the catchphrases? They charged Jacob *extra* every time they said them.

Jacob was broke by the end of the first week.

Finally, he had enough. He blew his whistle. *"Time-out! Family foul!"* he shouted. "None of you are acting like how you are on TV! Don't you understand? The people you portray on TV are wonderful. They bring laughter to the world. Don't you want to be better in real life?"

The actors shrugged. Janice (the mother) asked, "Does it pay more?"

"Actually, I'm out of money," Jacob said.

Jacob expected an *"Awwwwwwww!"* from the studio audience.

But there wasn't one.

The mob of snobby TV stars stomped out of his house and back into their limousines without a word.

Coach Jordan didn't even let Jacob keep the whistle.

Jacob didn't want to be Jacob Jordan anymore. He wanted to be Jacob *Jones* again.

So he sold his TV, got enough money to move his real parents back home, and swore off TV for the rest of his life.

Then he went and got himself a *free* library card.

CHAPTER 12
Olivia

More than anything, Olivia loved to learn. Even though she was still young, she wanted to stay in college as long as she could when she was older. So rather than spend any of her money, she put it all in the bank.

Why would she do such a thing?

Because college is very expensive. (Just ask your parents.)

CHAPTER 13
Classroom *13*

Like Santiago, Classroom 13 didn't get a dime either—even though it *was* there on the day Ms. Linda promised to share her winnings. The Classroom wasn't a student, but it had feelings, too—and its feelings were hurt.

The 13th Classroom vowed revenge on all the students one day....

CHAPTER 14
Ava

Ava was so excited when she got home with her check for $1,037,037,037.04, she asked her parents right away if she could start spending the money. They said, "No."

She spent it anyway.

If you know Ava, you know that she is a great friend. When William forgot his lunch one day, Ava shared her lunch with him. When Chloe spilled cranberry juice on her blouse before class photos, Ava lent her a sweater. And when Lily told her a secret, Ava promised not to tell anyone—and she didn't.

Ava wanted to share her newfound wealth with her friends. So she texted everyone and asked what she should spend the money on. The next day, she did exactly what would make her friends happy.

She bought an island—a *whole* island—in Hawaii. (Not one of the big ones, but one of the small ones.)

Ava built a huge castle on the island. The castle had everything her friends could think of: Tennis courts. Swimming pools. A movie theater. A dock with boats and Jet Skis. A ranch full of horses. It even had a waterslide park and cotton-candy machines.

She and her friends couldn't wait until it was ready. It took a while to build everything they wanted. But once it was done, Ava rented a private plane and flew everyone there.

For forty-seven hours, they had the most amazing time.

Then the ground started to shake. Puffs of black smoke began to burp out of the island mountain. The island's "director of fun" (who was actually Ava's mom, Heather) called Ava and said, "Hi, sweetie. I think maybe we should leave."

At first, Ava refused. But when the volcano erupted, she decided her mom was right. She and her friends (and all the horses) crammed onto her private jet and took off into the sky.

As they flew to safety, Ava looked out the window and watched her island sink beneath the surface of the ocean. "Oh well," she said. "At least now the fish have a cool place to hang out."

CHAPTER 15
Teo

Teo loved roller coasters, junk food, and fireworks. (He also loved dogs.) So when he got his check for $1,037,037,037.04, he wasn't sure how he was going to spend it. At least not until he realized that there was a certain amusement park that has roller coasters and junk food and daily fireworks shows.

Teo didn't even bother asking his parents if he could spend the money. He just started spending.

He called up the owners of this amusement park franchise and asked if he could buy it. They thought it was a prank call and hung up.

Teo called back. He asked again. They said, "No," then hung up.

Teo called back a third time and explained, "I have 1.037 billion dollars, and I would like to buy your amusement park."

"Oh! That's a lot of money. In that case, you can buy *one* of our theme parks."

"There's more than one?!" he asked.

"Of course!"

Teo ended up buying the one in Florida. He invited all his friends and cousins and uncles and aunts and grandparents for a week. (Even though he didn't want to, he finally told his parents they could come, too.)

For forty-seven hours, they rode roller coasters and ate too much junk food. Then ate more junk food and rode more roller coasters, until everyone had thrown up at least once on one of the rides. Except his dad, Luis, who had thrown up several times.

Teo, his friends, and his family didn't have to wait in any lines and all the food was free. (Well, it wasn't totally free. They still had to tip the waitstaff.) It was a truly amazing time. But the best part hadn't even happened yet. Teo was saving the best part for last—the fireworks show.

At the end of the second day, Teo demanded that the theme park have the biggest, brightest fireworks show they'd ever had in the history of fireworks shows. And they did. It turned out to be too much.

The world-famous amusement park burned down.

Teo was super annoyed for several days. Then he remembered he still had some money left: $37,037.04, to be exact. So he bought a German shepherd, a Siberian husky, and a new Xbox, and then took his family on a cruise. It was a really nice vacation.

CHAPTER 16
Earl

Remember how you thought I made a mistake on page 12? Well, I didn't.

The teacher (Ms. Linda) won $28 billion—that is, $28,000,000,000.

She agreed to *split it evenly* with each of her students (27 in total), minus one (Santiago, who was sick that day). That means 26 students.

If you add Ms. Linda, that's 27 people total.

So $28,000,000,000 divided by 27 is $1,037,037,037.04.

At the end of Chapter 2, I said: "Later that day, *twenty-five* students walked out of class with a check for over a billion dollars: $1,037,037,037.04 each, to be exact."

(Go on. Flip back to page 12 and check. See? I'm telling the truth. I'm Honest Lee.)

Did you notice? There were twenty-*six* students who won the lottery in the class, but only twenty-*five* students left that day. Why is that?

Simple. One of the "students" never left. You see, Earl lives in the classroom. Earl is a hamster.

During the first week of school, Ms. Linda counted her students. She had twenty-six in total. But all the kids insisted that the class pet, Earl the Hamster, was also a student.

Ms. Linda did not like arguing with her students, so she agreed. Earl became a student of Classroom 13 that day.

But how did Earl get the money? Well, he signed the contract, of course.

You see, Liam was something of a prankster—meaning he loved to pull pranks. And when he signed the contract for the lottery winnings, he thought he'd be funny and have Earl sign it, too. He colored the hamster's paw with a black marker and stamped it on the contract.

When it came time for everyone to collect their winnings, Liam explained it to Ms. Linda. "Well, if Earl signed the contract, then he's entitled to his share, too. After all, I am a woman of my word," she said.

So, yes, Earl received a check for $1,037,037,037.04.

What did he do with it? He shred it up with his cute little claws. Then he peed on it.

CHAPTER 17

Mark

Mark was the most handsome student in Classroom 13, and all the girls had a crush on him. But he only had eyes for one woman— Wonder Woman. Well, more specifically, Lynda Carter, the actress who played Wonder Woman in the 1970s TV show.

When he was little, he dreamed of guest-starring on the show and becoming friends with

Lynda. So when he won his lottery winnings, he knew *exactly* what he was going to do with his money. He would make his dream come true.

Mark hired a group of the world's most brilliant scientists (recommended to him by Triple J). Then he explained, "I want you to build me a time machine so I can go back in time to the 1970s."

"That is immoral!" one scientist said.

"It's dangerous!" said another.

"You could destroy the fabric of all space and time!" said a third.

Mark threw his money at them. All of it. Every dime. The scientists suddenly changed their tune.

"What a fantastic idea!" one scientist said.

"A brilliant use of money!" said another.

"Let's get started!" said a third.

So this group of scientists worked night and day for weeks until they had finally built a real-life time machine. "It'll only work *twice*," the scientists warned. "Once to go there, and once to come back. Got it?"

"Got it!" Mark said. He hopped inside and pushed the button. The whole world outside turned into bright light. The machine shook so hard, Mark thought his brains were going to poop out of his ears.

Instead, the time machine popped out on the set of *Wonder Woman*. "Who are you?" asked the director.

"I'm a time traveler from the future. I came back in time to see if I could be a guest star on the *Wonder Woman* TV show."

"Are you SAG?" the director asked.

"What's SAG?" Mark asked.

"Screen Actors Guild," the director said. "You can't be on TV unless you're part of the labor union."

Mark slapped himself in the face. He should have done a little more research before coming all the way back in time. He was so bummed. He wandered toward his time machine, kicking rocks as he went.

"Why the frown, kid?" someone asked.

Mark turned around. "Lynda Carter?!"

"That's me." She smiled with her perfect smile.

Mark suddenly didn't care about being on TV anymore. He had finally met his big crush. He explained everything that had happened. And then he and Lynda had a good laugh about it. She even taught him to do her Wonder Woman spin. Afterward, she autographed a black-and-white picture for him. She signed it *To my favorite time traveler. Love, Lynda.*

When Mark came home, back to the present day, he didn't have any more money, but he was the happiest boy in Classroom 13.

CHAPTER 18
Mya & Madison

Mya & Madison felt *twice* as lucky as everyone else in Classroom 13. This was because they were twins.

These twins had two of everything—two matching beds, two matching toothbrushes, two matching unicycles, and, yes, two matching checks for $1,037,037,037.04.

Some of the kids wondered if the sisters would combine their lottery winnings for a whopping

total of $2,074,074,074.08. That would make them *twice* as rich as everyone else.

But the twins didn't want to keep the money. They wanted to spend it.

As they almost always did, Mya & Madison had the exact same thought, at the exact same time: "We should each buy two of EVERY-THING and put it on a boat!" Mya & Madison said at the same time. "Like a Noah's Ark... *of stuff*!"

"But if we each buy *two* of the same thing, then we'll have *four* of everything—which is weird, because we're not quadruplets," Madison said.

"Ew. Quadruplets are weird," Mya said. "Well, if we each buy *one* of something, then together, we'll have *two* of everything!"

Mya & Madison smiled at the exact same time and said, "Then we'll have *twice* as much stuff as everybody else!"

The Ark of Stuff plan was a go.

Mya & Madison shopped until they dropped—

well, at least until their feet hurt. The girls went on a shopping spree, buying two of everything they'd ever wanted.

They bought two sequined pantsuits, two bedazzled cell phones, two glittered swimming pools, two emerald-crusted backpacks, two diamond-covered bicycles, two opal Hula-Hoops, two golden trampolines, and so on. (If there was anything shiny and expensive, they had two of it.)

Then, using their father's top secret military connections, the girls bought two aircraft carriers and had all their high-priced items flown there in helicopters.

The twins wanted to show off their spend-ings. So they planned a huge party on the ships and invited all their classmates from Classroom 13. Unfortunately, before the celebration, their ships were so heavy, they sank.

Because they were twins, Mya & Madison felt *twice* as sad about their loss.

CHAPTER 19
Dev

Dev's whole life revolved around video games. He'd go to sleep playing his PlayStation and move over to the Xbox when he woke up. On his way to school, he played his portable Nintendo. He also had over a hundred games on his phone for playing in between—and sometimes *during*—bathroom breaks.

"Are you pooping or playing video games in there?!" his dad would yell at the bathroom door.

"Both!" Dev answered.

So when Dev got his check for over a billion dollars, he knew what he wanted—to level up to *VIRTUAL REALITY*.

(His thumbs were getting tired of all the button mashing anyway.)

A store-bought VR system was *not* going to cut it for Dev. He wanted to live his life *inside* the most sophisticated virtual-reality world money could buy. So he found the greatest video game designers in the world and hired them.

"I want to *live* in a video game world," Dev said.

"For how long?" one game designer asked.

"*Forever,*" Dev said.

"But what about sleeping, or eating?" another game designer asked. "Or you know, going number one, or...you know, number two..."

"I'll be doing everything in this game world," Dev said. Then he handed his check over to the game designers. "Now get coding!"

The game designers worked twenty-four hours a day, seven days a week, to finish Dev's Virtual World in just one month. Many nights, they skipped sleeping to make Dev's deadline. To meet his demands, they skipped over some *tiny details*, but they could always add stuff later.

"Are you done yet?!" Dev snapped.

"Not quite," the designers said. "We need to add a Save function."

"Don't bother," Dev said. "I'm never leaving this game."

Dev stepped into the VR suit and turned on his new world. He couldn't believe his eyes.

The virtual reality was so crisp and so clear, it was like being in the real world—only way better because it wasn't real. In VR, Dev could fly like Superman. He could build castles with a wave of his virtual glove. He could fight monsters, drive race cars and rockets, and shoot up killer robots. He could even nap on a virtual cloud.

And when he had to use the restroom...well, he just went wherever. (The VR suit took care of the...*stuff*.)

Dev's VR was everything he could ever dream of and more. He ate virtual pizzas, rode virtual roller coasters, went on virtual quests, and met virtual friends from his favorite video games. In his game, there was no school and no chores and no nagging parents. And best of all, every day was an adventure.

Out of nowhere, Dev could kinda, sorta hear someone yelling (from back in the real world). He didn't want to deal with it, whatever it was. He wanted to play his game. With his glove, Dev turned up the volume. Now all he could hear was the cool techno music of his latest mission.

Suddenly, the virtual world around him vanished. There was nothing but black in every direction, until a blinking red light appeared overhead. Big capital letters appeared in the VR:

NO SAVE FILE FOUND. PROGRESS LOST.

Dev removed his VR goggles, returning to the *real* world. He was ready to shout at the VR game programmers. Instead, he screamed. He was surrounded by electrical sparks and a small fire.

FWWSSSSSHHHHHHH!

The programmers sprayed him (and the VR suit) down with fire extinguishers. "What happened?!" Dev cried.

"Sorry, little dude," one of the programmers said. "The system overheated and caught fire."

"But the game is okay, right?"

The VR programmers shook their head.

Dev sighed. It was officially *Game Over* for Dev's Virtual World. Now he was stuck in reality like the rest of the people on the planet.

CHAPTER 20
Ethan

Ethan Earhart's parents were both lawyers. He hoped one day to grow up to be just like them. Ham or turkey? Paper or plastic? Boxers or briefs? Everything was something that could be argued. And he loved to argue.

"Six times nine is fifty-four," Ms. Linda said.

"Objection!" Ethan yelled.

"This is *not* a courtroom, Ethan. This is math.

Numbers don't lie. Six times nine *is* fifty-four."

"But how do we know that for sure? That numbers don't lie? Isn't a one lying about being an *odd* number? It does not look at all odd to me. In fact, it looks rather normal. One might say it looks fair, or *even*! But ten? Ten looks odd!"

"That's not how that works," Ms. Linda said.

"I disagree."

"That doesn't prove that numbers lie."

"I beg to differ."

Ethan was not doing this to be rude. Quite the contrary, Ethan was trying to be *judicious*—which meant showing good sense.

"No, it doesn't," Ethan said.

"Yes, it does," I (Honest Lee) said back.

"I beg to differ."

"Well, let's agree to disagree—hey, wait! Why are you debating with *me*?" I said. "*I'm* the narrator. Argue with your friends. I'm just a voice in this book!"

Anyway.

After Ethan found he had $1,037,037,037.04 to spend, his first idea was to buy a hot-air balloon. After all, he'd always wanted to fly in one. (Ethan was in a wheelchair, but he wouldn't let that stop him from seeing the world, or becoming the world's best lawyer.)

But as usual, Ethan began a list of pros and cons for buying a hot-air balloon.

Pros: Flight. Seeing the land from up high. Cool story.

Cons: Height. Falling to my death. Birds trying to steal my lunch.

Over the next few days, Ethan argued with himself. He was so stuck on this topic that he went back and forth and back and forth, arguing both sides of *buying* a hot-air balloon and *not buying* a hot-air balloon. He asked other students their thoughts.

"Buy a comic!" Fatima said.

"Buy a cat!" Emma said.

"Buy a fart!" Liam said.

"No, I don't want any of those," Ethan said. "Especially that last one."

After days without sleep, Ethan found himself yelling, "Objection!" at himself. Finally, he found one more pro than con. And that settled it.

He bought a hot-air balloon.

That weekend, Ethan withdrew the remaining $1,036,987,037.04 and loaded it into the balloon's passenger basket. Before boarding himself, he debated (with himself) about whether he should fly east or west first. And of course, that debate took a good, long while.

While Ethan argued with himself, the balloon broke away—with his money, but without him. A strong gust of wind caught the balloon and blew it up into the air.

"Hey, that's my balloon!" Ethan yelled. (But then argued with himself, "Is it, though, or does the balloon own itself?")

Ethan watched as his hot-air balloon—and his fortune—disappeared into the clouds.

The balloon made global headlines the next day. Apparently, every time the wind blew, the sky rained money. All over the world, people watched for the money balloon, calling it "a wonderful, beautiful miracle."

Ethan begged to differ.

CHAPTER 21
Chloe

Is there a canned good in your house that you don't know what to do with? Do you know someone who likes meals delivered to their home? Perhaps you want to save the dolphins, but don't know where to start?

Well, just ask Chloe. Chloe cares. About *everything*.

Chloe Canter never met a cause she didn't

want to take up. She organized four blood drives and twelve fund-raisers last year. She raised awareness about deforestation by chaining herself to a tree. When Classroom 13 needed a new water bottle for the class hamster, she hosted a telethon.

(She raised over six hundred dollars. For a tiny bottle. For a hamster.)

That's *how much* Chloe cares.

Naturally, Chloe already knew where her lottery money was going when Ms. Linda wrote her a check. Her winnings were going straight to CHARITY.

But how would she divide up the money? There were so many charities that needed her help: The one that gave free diapers to single moms. The one that built schools in poor countries. The one that set aside land for lions. Even the one that taught street kids how to steal nicer clothes. (That is a charity, isn't it?)

"You should give it all to one charity," Ava said. "That would make a big difference."

"You should give a little bit to every charity that exists," Teo said. "That will make lots of little differences."

"You should just fart on it," Liam blurted, making a loud fart noise.

Chloe ignored Liam. She considered Ava's and Teo's suggestions. She finally decided she wanted to make a big difference. But which charity would she select?

Chloe thought hard. The lottery winnings came to her at random. So that was how she should donate the money.

Chloe went online and found a list of every major charity on the planet. There were over 1.5 million charities in the United States alone. So she closed her eyes, scrolled down through the webpage, and let her mouse land on a random charity.

She opened her eyes. "National Flatulence

Awareness, a nonprofit," she read. "What's *flatulence?*"

Liam's eyes grew wide. "It means *fart!*"

Chloe thought Liam was kidding, so she looked it up. "Flatulence" did, in fact, mean intestinal gas, which is what a fart is.

Chloe shrugged. If fate wanted her to use her winnings to make America more aware of farts, then that's what she had to do. *Farts have feelings, too,* she thought.

She phoned the Flatulence Awareness hotline and made her donation. The woman on the other end of the phone nearly fainted. "Thank you! Bless you, my child!" Chloe heard the woman pass gas on the other end of the phone. "I apologize. I expel gas when I am excited."

That night, Chloe felt good. She had made a real difference in the world. She was warming up to the idea of educating people through National Flatulence Awareness, when a public service announcement on TV came on. An oil tanker crashed off the coast of a place called Penguin Cove. Oil was everywhere.

A single tear leaked out from behind Chloe's glasses and down her cheek.

"Oh no!" she said, running to the phone. She called the Flatulence Awareness hotline. "Earlier today, I donated over a billion dollars, and I'm afraid I made a mistake. I need the money back—not for me, of course. But for the oil-coated penguins! You know, for a *real* charity."

After a long *pooooooooot*, the woman said, "Pardon me. I expel gas when I am offended."

"Why are you offended?" Chloe asked.

"Because your change of heart really *stinks*."

Chloe didn't know how to respond to that.

"Ah, I see," the woman said. "The silent but deadly treatment. Well, the money is gone. And there's nothing that can be done. She who dealt it...well, you know how the rest goes. Good day, ma'am."

CHAPTER 22
Fatima

All the kids in Classroom 13 knew one thing about Fatima: She had "issues."

No, not *someone-call-the-cops-on-that-girl* kind of "issues." I mean, actual *issues*...of comic books. Fatima Farooq was a comic book collector with a rather serious collection. She bought two of every comic: one to read and a second that remained—perfectly safe and in mint condition—in a plastic slipcover, inside a protective box, never to be touched by human hands.

I bet you can guess what she bought with her share of the lottery winnings.

(What? Who said a refrigerator? Yes, you did. I heard you. Now stop talking back to this book or people are going to think *you* have "issues.")

Fatima used her lottery winnings to buy every comic book ever made. Even the super-rare ones owned by pale old men who swore they'd never part with their most-prized possessions.

She bought *classic* issues, *deluxe* issues, *autographed* issues, *misprinted* issues, and issues with *die-cut holographic foil*. She bought superhero comics, ninja comics, monster comics, robot comics, sci-fi comics, and old cartoon comic strips that were hanging up in a comic book museum in another state.

Fatima bought them all, spending every last cent.

Her mother did *not* approve.

"Fatima Farooq!" her mom yelled from deep within the stacks and stacks of comic books that now lined every square inch of their house. "What is all this?!"

"My comic book collection!" she yelled back. "It's finally complete."

With all the stacks of comics and mountains of boxes and layers of protective plastic everywhere, it took Mrs. Farooq six grueling days to dig a tunnel to her daughter's bedroom. Mrs. Farooq wore full climbing gear, including a little helmet with a light on it. Her face was covered in brightly colored stains (from smudging the pages along the way), and her hands were shaking.

"What have I told you about comic books?" Mrs. Farooq growled.

"But, Mom—" Fatima said. "I have some educational comics, too! Look," she pleaded, pulling out an issue to show. "This guy *learned* how to melt minds with a mind-melting laser! Know-ledge *is* power!"

Mrs. Farooq was not amused. "What have I told you...?"

Fatima repeated her mother's words. "Comics are bad news..."

"And..."

"And young, vulnerable minds shouldn't be reading them," Fatima and her mom said together.

Mrs. Farooq took out her phone and started dialing.

The next morning, a fleet of garbage trucks rolled up to Fatima's house. Soon, her billion-dollar comic collection—the biggest one in the world, I'm told—would fill landfills across the country. And birds would poop on it.

Honest Lee does NOT agree with Mrs. Farooq. Comics are NOT bad news. They are GREAT, and everyone should read them.

CHAPTER 23
Yuna

Ask anyone: Yuna is a *mystery*.

Much to the annoyance of her classmates—and Ms. Linda—Yuna speaks only in code. Instead of words, Yuna uses numbers to communicate. The numbers correspond to each letter in the alphabet. Meaning:

A = 1

B = 2

C = 3

D = 4

E = 5

And so on...counting upward until you reach the letter Z, which of course equals 26.

What's that? You want to know what Yuna did with her money? Well, all I'm going to say is what she told me:

25-21-14-1 8-9-4 8-5-18
13-15-14-5-25 19-15-13-5-23-8-5-18-5
19-5-3-18-5-20.
19-15 19-5-3-18-5-20, 19-8-5
6-15-18-7-15-20 23-8-5-18-5 9-20 23-1-19.

CHAPTER 24
Benji

Benji had very BIG—or should I say, very *small*—plans for his new fortune.

"I'm going to *shrink* them all!" he told his parents. Benji was smiling ear to ear. His mom and dad were nervous, until they realized he wasn't talking about shrinking every *person* in the world.

He was talking about shrinking their *pets*.

You see, Benji had two loves: football and

animals. He loved animals, but he loved *minia-ture* animals even more: Panda cows and micro pigs. Bee hummingbirds and Philippine tarsiers. And let's not forget miniature horses and teensy-weensy fennec foxes. (I blame the Internet, and all its videos of tiny, itty-bitty animals that are cuter than cute.)

Benji had a stuffed animal collection (on the same shelf as his football trophies), but it just wasn't the same. He wanted real-life mini pets. He wanted to hold them and hug them and love them and live happily ever after.

Have you ever seen a pygmy marmoset? (Look it up.) It's no bigger than the palm of your hand. It could live in your shirt pocket. Benji wanted one. And he wanted everyone to have one. Everyone deserved a little bit of minia-ture joy.

"Think about it," Benji told his parents. "If everyone had a teacup puppy to carry around all day, no one would be sad. You can't be sad when you look at that tiny, furry cuteness with its big, beautiful eyes. Plus, they're perfect for football practice—you can pull them out and cuddle with them in between plays."

Benji's parents didn't understand their son.

Triple J and Mark recommended the same scientists who helped them. "They *really* like money. Like, way *more* than they like obeying the laws of nature and space-time and whatnot. If you're willing to pay, they'll pretty much do whatever you want."

So Benji hired the scientists to build him a *shrink ray*. It looked like a huge laser cannon from an old sci-fi movie. Once charged, it shot a beam that could miniaturize *anything*.

"Big, scary animals become tiny, cutesy animals," said one scientist.

"Extra cutesy!" another scientist added, counting his money.

"How can I be sure it works?" Benji asked.

Just then, a shrunken scientist the size of an action figure climbed onto his shoulder. "Trust me," his wee voice squeaked, "*it works*."

Benji was so excited to get started, he bought two local pet stores, a farm, and the nearest zoo.

One by one, Benji put the animals in front of the shrink ray. He pulled the lever and watched them shrink down to the size of an apple. He could hardly believe it—petting and holding each of the impossibly tiny animals made him smile so hard, it hurt. (But in a good way.)

With each new animal, he knocked another wish off his wish list. Pygmy marmosets in his shirt pocket? Check. Walking a miniature horse on a leash? Done-zo. Teacup puppies nestled safely in his gym bag for halftime cuddles? Mission accomplished.

Benji invited Classroom 13 to his miniature zoo. He reminded everyone, "Be careful where you step!"

His fellow students lost their minds. Everyone wanted one. And Benji wanted everyone to be able to have the same kind of strange love that he had. So he planned to open his zoo to the public and give one animal away to anyone who wanted one. Unfortunately, before he could start giving away his tiny animals (and help the world to find love and happiness), several things happened all at once:

1. The local pet stores got together and sued Benji for making impossibly cute animals. They couldn't compete with that. Local law enforcement took away Benji's shrink ray until the trial was settled.

2. PETA (People for the Ethical Treatment of Animals) protested his new zoo and his giving away animals to anyone who wanted them. They thought everyone should be screened. Their lawyers also sued Benji. His zoo was closed to the public until the trial was settled.

3. His parents sat him down when he came

home. They also had their lawyers with them. "You've shrunk enough things for now," his mom's lawyer said. "Time to *grow* your bank account."

"Your parents put the rest of your money in a savings account," the lawyers said. "That way, it can collect interest."

"But what about helping the world find love through miniature pets? It could bring world peace!"

"Your dreams will have to wait until you're older," his mom's lawyer said.

"When?" he asked.

"When you're eighteen," the lawyers said.

Benji was upset that he couldn't help the rest of the world find miniature happiness. But for now, at least, Benji was happy. When the cops and lawyers weren't looking, Benji managed to sneak a handful of plum-sized pets into his pockets....

CHAPTER 25
Preeya

Preeya is best friends with Olivia Ogilvy. (You know, the girl who put all her money in the bank for college instead of having fun with it.)

Sorry. I mean: Preeya *was* best friends with Olivia. (Past tense.)

Why aren't they best friends anymore? Well, Preeya's mom is friends with Olivia's mom, and you know how moms like to share *everything*.

At their weekly poker night, Olivia's mom said, "Oh goodness. I am so proud of Olivia for putting all her lottery money away for college."

That night, Preeya's mom went straight home and said, "Preeya, give me your lottery check. We're going straight to the bank to deposit it into your college fund—just like Olivia did."

Preeya was *not* happy. She didn't want to save her money for college. She wanted to spend it *now*. She planned to use her money to become famous so that she could win the heart of a certain famous male pop star—you know the one: super cute, super talented, sings love songs that make your heart swell (even though you tell everyone you *don't* like his music, even though secretly you *do*).

Preeya was furious.

But maybe—hopefully—she'll be more appreciative when she's older.

(I doubt it.)

CHAPTER 26
Liam

The students of Classroom 13 have always wondered: How is it that *little* Liam is able to make such *big* farts?

Liam's gas ranged from silent-but-deadly to trombone-loud-but-without-a-smell. It was quite the talent.

Mason guessed he ate chili for breakfast, lunch, and dinner. Triple J guessed he trained with an order of butt-blasting monks in Tibet.

Ximena guessed he was simply born with a gift for gas.

The truth was...*practice*. After all, practice makes perfect. And Liam, the class prankster, worked very hard to create controlled farts, which he used for comedic effect. His favorite phrase was: "Pull my finger."

If he tells you to do this—trust me—*don't*.

Liam tried to get laughs to distract others from how *small* and *short* he was. He did not like being the smallest student in Classroom 13. He dreamed *big*. In fact, he's always dreamed of being in the *Global Book of World Records*.

So when he won the lottery, he decided to spend his $1,037,037,037.04 on making his dreams come true. How? Well, he liked pranking people, but that was no way to get a world record. But he did like eating. (No matter how much he ate, he never gained weight thanks to a very fast metabolism.)

Finally, he decided on a worthy world record— Most Desserts Ever Eaten by a Human Being.

Liam planned on spending his fortune devouring every kind of sweet treat imaginable and going down in history for it.

Liam phoned the Global World Record office and informed them of his plan. They sent two representatives to join Liam on his world travels. Dan and Dana would follow Liam with a camera and a journal to document his progress.

The journey began in Switzerland, home to the world's finest chocolatiers. Liam sampled thousands of varieties of chocolate in one sitting and washed it all down with molten liquid cocoa from a chocolate fountain.

Dan and Dana gave a thumbs-up and said, "Good start."

In Russia, Liam ate truckloads of Kiev cake. In South Africa, he spooned malva pudding down his throat. In Brazil, he consumed tres leches cakes. In Belgium, Liam devoured chocolate chip waffles. He licked up liquid nitrogen ice cream in Manila and ais kacang in Malaysia.

In Australia, he forked in lamingtons. In Japan, he inhaled trays of green tea mochi. In Turkey, Liam swallowed pans of baklava. In Hawaii, he ate haupia delights until he couldn't take another bite. He ate deep-fried candy bars in Scotland and then chocolate-covered chapulines in Mexico. (You should probably *not* look up what *chapulines* are....)

(I told you not *to look them up.)*

Finally, Liam went to Paris to eat the world's most expensive dessert: a seventy-seven-scoop sundae covered in gold dust and real diamonds. Once he finished, he would be a Global World Record holder.

He began to shovel the dessert down his throat. Four spoonfuls from finishing, Liam got light-headed and his stomach began to rumble. "Can I have some water?" he asked Dan and Dana. "I'm not feeling so—"

Liam keeled over and *died*.

It's okay. It was only for a few seconds.

Dan and Dana were not just judges. They were also certified paramedics. They zapped Liam with heart paddles. Twenty thousand volts of electricity surged through Liam's veins—along with massive amounts of sugar and dairy.

As Liam came back to life, he let out the loudest, most powerful, earth-rumbling fart a human body had ever produced. The entire restaurant shook.

As the Global World Record reps helped him to sit up, Liam said, "I think I'm done with sweets."

Liam did *not* break the record for Most Desserts Ever Eaten by a Human Being. But he *did* break the record for Most Powerful Fart Ever Farted by a Human Being.

Dan and Dana noted: "The shock wave of the fart was felt as far away as Spain. It was seismic!"

Liam could live with that.

CHAPTER 27
Isabella

Isabella Inglebel loved horses.

To no one's surprise, Isabella bought herself the biggest horse ranch in America. How many horses can $1,037,037,037.04 buy you?

Well, it depends on the age, health, fame, and breed of the horse. But all in all, Isabella bought exactly 312,462 horses.

Now Isabella Inglebel owns 312,462 horses.

Or, I should say, *owned* 312,462 horses. (Past tense.)

You see, Isabella's hired horseman—an old cowboy named Old Blue—told her she needed a fence for her horses. But Isabella didn't want her beloved pets to feel fenced in. She wanted them to run free.

And they ran free all right.

All those wild horses galloped off into the sunset, never to return. No amount of carrots or apples or hay could lure them back. Isabella should have listened to Old Blue.

CHAPTER 28

Hugo

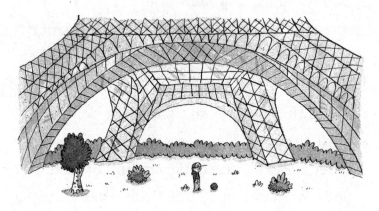

Hugo Houde est né et a grandi à Paris. Quand Hugo avait dix ans, sa famille a dû partir vivre à l'étranger pour le travail de son père. C'est ainsi qu'Hugo a atterri dans la classe numéro treize où personne ne parlait français.

La France lui manquait énormément. Comme il ne pouvait pas y retourner, il décida d'amener la France à lui. Alors, avec son argent, il acheta la tour Eiffel et la mit dans son jardin. C'est la vie.

CHAPTER 29
Zoey

Unlike her classmates, Zoey was not in a hurry to spend her winnings. She was already rich, so all she wanted to do was cash the check and bring all the money back to her house. She wanted to be surrounded by the cash.

So Zoey did just that.

An entire fleet of armored cars full of cash followed her home from the bank. When they pulled into her driveway, the guards asked,

"Where do you want this?"

Zoey hadn't thought about it. Then she remembered seeing a cartoon about a greedy duck. He had so much money, he could jump off a diving board and swim around in it, like a swimming pool.

Zoey liked that. She wouldn't have to spend the money, but it wouldn't just be sitting around gathering dust either.

"In the backyard," Zoey said. "Put the money in the pool!"

The guards unzipped the bags and dumped the stacks of cash into her swimming pool—right into the water.

"You're going to ruin that money," her dad said.

Zoey ignored him.

Her dad shrugged and let Zoey do as she wanted. After all, it was *her* money.

She ran inside to put on her bathing suit and swim goggles.

Once Zoey's entire fortune was in the pool, she somersaulted off her trampoline and into the pool of money.

Ker-splash—CRASH!

With so much soggy paper, the water didn't feel very good when she dove in. In fact, it felt like diving into the shallow end of a pool. Zoey knocked up her elbows and knees rather badly.

She didn't care, though. She wanted to swim in money. But swimming through the cash-filled water was like swimming through oatmeal. If that weren't bad enough, all the dollar bills made it tough to see underwater. Zoey swam right into the pool's wall and bumped her head.

After a few minutes, she noticed that her red hair was turning green. But worse, the cash was dissolving into mush. Her fortune was melting.

"Dad! Dad! What's happening to my money?!" she screamed.

"I told you it would ruin the money," her dad said. "This morning, the pool man treated

the water with special cleaning chemicals—chemicals strong enough to destroy the leaves at the bottom of the pool."

Or anything else paper thin for that matter, I should add.

Zoey leaped out of the pool and watched her fortune disintegrate into green soup. She stormed inside, upset and penniless.

She cried as she took a bubble bath—in regular, plain old water—just like normal (poor) people.

CHAPTER 30
Really Unlucky Ms. Linda

Lucky Ms. Linda's luck was about to change. (Again.)

Ms. Linda was having a wonderful day. She'd had a very pricey brunch ($2,000 for scrambled eggs and toast). Her anti-bird shampoo made her hair shine and bounce like a supermodel's ($20,000 a bottle). And she was about to buy her dream house—the most expensive estate in the state ($200,000,000).

"All you have to do is sign here," the real estate agent said, "and the mansion will be yours."

Ms. Linda looked at the sky to see if there were any thunderclouds. (There weren't.) It was a beautiful and sunny day. She breathed a sigh of relief. She signed the contract and shook the real estate agent's hand.

"Congratulations on your new home!" he said.

Ms. Linda stepped into her beautiful dream house and squealed a happy squeal. She was unaware of a slight rumble beneath her.

Ms. Linda spent every last dime of her fortune to make the house *perfect*. She hired Emma's parents (the "interior decorators") to tell her exactly what furniture to buy. They helped her order rugs from countries she could not pronounce and purchase silverware from the fanciest stores in New York City. She even purchased the famous *Mona Lisa* painting by Da Vinci and hung it in her living room.

The house was everything Ms. Linda had dreamed of and more...

...which is why Ms. Linda tried to ignore the odd things. For example, no matter how many times she got them fixed, her floors remained uneven. The countertops were also not right. If she put a plate on the counter, the dish would slide off and shatter onto the floor.

She called the real estate agent. He said, "Oh, that. It's just the house settling."

One day, Ms. Linda nearly broke her leg, falling into the driveway. It seemed her front porch had risen six feet above the sidewalk. This made getting in and out of her house a real challenge.

She called the real estate agent. He said, "Oh, that. Watch your step."

When she tried to host a dinner party for some of the other teachers, her house began to creak and shake. It was so noticeable that her friends asked, "Is it haunted?"

"No, no," Ms. Linda said. "My house just has a lot of personality."

One sunny day, Ms. Linda decided on a quiet game of croquet in her front yard. She raised the mallet and hit the ball. When the ball struck her house, the ground caved in and swallowed her house whole.

Ms. Linda peered into the pit in the ground. She saw her fancy furniture and beautiful dishes and the *Mona Lisa*—all destroyed. Her dream home had been swallowed up by a *sinkhole*.

Good thing Ms. Linda was smart enough to get insurance.

"I'm sorry, ma'am," said the insurance adjuster. "The sinkhole that destroyed your home is *not* covered by your insurance."

Several birds dove at Ms. Linda to pull at her hair. She tried to swat them away but quickly gave up.

Everything in Classroom 13 returned to the way it was before Ms. Linda won the lottery. Life was normal again. Well, as *normal* as Classroom 13 gets.

Ms. Linda was still late to class, Santiago was still sick, Hugo was still French, and Earl was still a hamster. Triple J may or may not have had clones running around. Yuna still didn't know where her fortune was. And Mason's best friend was still a crossing guard that gave him fresh milk every morning.

The truth be told: Winning lots of money—and losing lots of money—hadn't changed anyone's lives all that much.

In fact, no one in Classroom 13 had really learned *anything*.

What a shame.

Did you learn anything?

No? I didn't think you would. Honestly.

CHAPTER 31
Your Chapter

That's right—it's your turn!

Grab some paper and a writing utensil. (Not a fork, silly. Try a pencil or pen.) Or if you have one of those fancy computer doo-hickeys, use that. Now tell me...

If you won the lottery
what would *YOU* do with the money?!

When you're done, share it with your teacher, your family, and your friends. (Don't forget your pets! Pets like to hear stories, too.) You can even ask your parents to send me your chapter at the address below.

HONEST LEE

LITTLE, BROWN BOOKS FOR YOUNG READERS

1290 Avenue of the Americas

New York, NY 10104

Disastrous

THE MAGICAL WISHES OF CLASSROOM 13

By **Honest Lee** & **Matthew J. Gilbert**
Art by **Joelle Dreidemy**

LITTLE, BROWN AND COMPANY
New York ☆ Boston

★ CONTENTS ★

Psst! Hey you. Yes, you, the reader. Earl (the class hamster) suggests using a mirror for Yuna's code. You're welcome.

CHAPTER 1
Wishless Ms. Linda

When *wishless* schoolteacher Ms. Linda LaCrosse woke up Thursday morning, she decided it would be another unfortunate day. And she was right.

First, she washed her hair with toothpaste, then brushed her teeth with shampoo and conditioner. It did *not* taste good—but her hair was minty fresh. When she got in her car, she realized it was out of gas. So she had to walk to work. On her way, the wind grew rather strong. It blew her down, and she scraped her knee. She wished that she had a wish (that would come true). But she didn't have any wishes.

I did mention she was wish*less*.

Ms. Linda was almost to work, when she noticed a giant hole in the sidewalk. It appeared that someone had been digging. *Probably mole people*, she thought.

As she was walking around the hole, a large gust of wind came along. It blew her so hard, she fell backward into the hole.

Bonk! She fell right on her bottom. Halfway buried in the rubble beside her, she saw a golden lamp.

This was not the kind of lamp you plug in to light a room. It was an ancient oil lamp that could light up a room if you filled it with oil and lit it. (An oil lamp was one of the ways people saw at night a long time ago. Of course, then some wise guy went and invented electricity and put all the oil lamps out of business.)

"What an odd place to put a lamp," Ms. Linda noted. She pulled the golden lamp out of the dirt and examined it. "It's quite beautiful, though. I'll take it to school and show my classroom. We can talk about other things one can find in the ground—rocks, worms, dinosaur bones.... Yes, what a great lesson!"

As she crawled out of the hole, Ms. Linda thought her day was starting to look up. Then, several bees started to chase her. She was only partially allergic and would not die. But bee stings still hurt. Ms. Linda knew, because bees loved to sting her. She had been stung one hundred and seventy-three times. And that was just this year.

The bees chased her all the way to the school. When she got inside, she slammed the door shut and watched all the bees bop against the glass. "Ha! You didn't get me!" Ms. Linda said. But one bee had flown ahead to wait for her inside the school. It stung her right on the lip.

"Ow! Ow! Ow!" Ms. Linda cried.

"You're late again, Ms. Linda," said the principal, pointing to his watch.

"Sawwy, Mistew Pwincipaw," Ms. Linda said. She could no longer pronounce her *r*'s or her *l*'s because her lip was swollen.

She rushed down the hall in her heels—*click clack, click clack, click clack*—all the way to her classroom. Her classroom was number 13, which, if you don't know, is a very *un*lucky number.

"Oh, students, I apowogize *tewwibwy* fow being *tewwibwy* wate," Ms. Linda said. "I've had quite the awfuw mowning!"

Of her twenty-seven students (including Earl the Hamster), twenty-five of them were present.

Santiago "Sniffles" Santos was not at school. He had a terrible flu. He begged his mom to let him go to school so he didn't miss anything fun, but she insisted he stay home.

William was also not in class. He had told his grandma he had a stomachache so he could stay home. But he did *not* have a stomachache. He just wanted to stay home all day and watch cartoons.

Of the twenty-five students who were in class, only twenty-two of them were awake. Of those twenty-two, seven were on their phones. Of the fifteen left, two were arguing (over something dumb) and three were drawing Jedi lightsabers (which are not dumb at all).

Of the ten students left, four were playing a card game, three were flying drones, two were studying for today's quiz, and one was running in circles. (You might think I'm talking about Earl, but I am not.)

Out of all twenty-five students present, none of them were happy to see Ms. Linda. They all *liked* Ms. Linda (especially after she gave them each a check for over a billion dollars), but they did not want to *see* Ms. Linda. Not today. Her lips were swollen to the size of two bananas, and she'd broken out into a terrible rash.

She looked quite monstrous.

"Ms. Linda!" Ava said, covering her eyes. "What happened to your face?"

"Are you turning into a zombie?" Teo asked.

"I am not tuwning into a zombie," Ms. Linda explained. "I am pawtiawwy awwewgic to bee stings, and I was stung this mowning."

"Ew," said Mya.

"Gross," said Madison.

"*Votre visage est horrible!*" shouted Hugo, who was from France and spoke only in French.

"That's enough, chiwdwen," Ms. Linda said. "Wet's not waste anymowe time. You'we hewe to *weawn*, and I am *hewe* to teach. Today I found a *gowden wamp*."

"You mean a golden lamp," corrected Olivia.

"That's what I said, a *gowden wamp*," repeated Ms. Linda.

Ms. Linda pulled the golden lamp out of her purse. When the students saw it, they were already bored. "That lamp doesn't even have a plug," said Mark. "How's it supposed to work?"

"We*ww*, *wet* me exp*wain*," Ms. Linda started. Noticing how dirty the lamp was, she gave it a hard rub with the palm of her hand. There was a loud crack of lightning and a *poof* of purple smoke—then a ghostly blue man appeared, floating in the middle of the classroom.

CHAPTER 2
Wishful Ms. Linda

Schoolteacher Ms. Linda LaCrosse and the children of Classroom 13 stared at the blue man. He was *floating* in the middle of Classroom 13 as if he were a cloud. The students could see through him a little, like a dirty window. Also, he smelled kind of bad, like a fart after eating chili for lunch.

"Um, excuse me," Ms. Linda spoke up. "Who

awe you?!" Because of her swollen lip, she still couldn't pronounce *l*'s or *r*'s.

"I am the Grand Djinn," the blue man said.

"What's a gin?" Sophia asked.

"Well, a cotton gin is a machine that separates cotton fibers from their seeds," said Olivia. She was the smartest student in the 13th Classroom.

"So you make clothes?" Sophia asked.

"No, I grant wishes," said the djinn. "I am a djinn, not a gin."

"Oh, you mean a genie!" said Ethan.

"I am *not* a genie; I am a djinn!" said the djinn. "'Genie' is a dumb word that some silly Frenchman made up while translating Arabic in the mid-seventeenth century."

"*Comment osez-vous?!*" said Hugo, offended.

"Sounds like a genie to me," said Jacob.

"I am a djinn!" the djinn thundered.

"No need to get *gwumpy*. Wouwd you *wike* a juice box?" Ms. Linda poked a straw through the

foil hole and gave it to the blue man. The djinn drank it happily.

"Now, couwd you *teww* me why you'*we* hewe?" Ms. Linda asked with her swollen lip.

"I don't understand," the djinn asked. "Why are you talking funny?"

"Oh, dawn it! A bee stung me this mowning, and now I'm not tawking *wight*. I wish this swowwen wip wouwd go away."

"Wish granted!" the djinn said, snapping his fingers. A swirl of gold magic flew through the air and hit Ms. Linda in the lip. Her lip immediately shrank and returned to normal.

"WOW!" the whole class said in awe.

"Does Ms. Linda get more wishes?" asked Ava.

"Do all of us get wishes?" asked Teo.

"I suppose each of you can have *one* wish," the djinn said.

"Genies give three wishes!" shouted Liam.

"I am not a genie; I am a djinn. And you watch

too many movies. In the real world, a djinn only grants a person one wish. So think carefully."

Ms. Linda got very excited. She had always wanted a wish. She knew exactly what she would wish for. "As the teacher, I think I should make my wish first," she said. "That way, the students can see how to make a good wish."

"Sorry," the djinn said. "You already used your wish—on your lip."

Ms. Linda sat down and put her head on the desk. She took three deep breaths, then stood up. She would be sad later. Right now she needed to be a good teacher. "Okay, class. Listen up. Everyone gets one wish. But we will do this one student at a time. The djinn may be very cruel in not giving me another wish, but he is still a guest in our classroom. When I call your name, you can come up and tell Mr. Djinn your wish."

The kids were all buzzing with excitement. They couldn't wait for their turn.

CHAPTER 3
Isabella

Isabella sat all the way in the back of the classroom by the hamster, so she was often last in line. But today, by some strange stroke of good luck, she managed to be the first in line to ask the ~~genie~~ djinn for a wish—and she knew *exactly* what she wanted.

"I wish for a UNICORN!" Isabella said.

"How original," the djinn said, rolling his eyes. After a burst of magic, a unicorn appeared.

Isabella was the happiest horse-loving girl in the world...for about a day. After taking the mythical beast home, she soon realized *just how different* unicorns are from normal horses.

First, she tried to feed it. The unicorn didn't want hay or apples or carrots to eat. The unicorn became so *hangry* (hungry + angry), it smashed through the wall of her house with its sparkly horn. It destroyed her mom's kitchen, hunting for what it really wanted: fresh-baked cupcakes with pink icing and sprinkles that Isabella's mom had made that morning. The unicorn devoured them and was happy.

Isabella's mom, however, was *not*. Surrounded by complete destruction, she cried and cried. "That horned pony destroyed my fine wedding china!"

But that wasn't all.

Isabella's unicorn did not like to bathe in water. It insisted on washing itself with glitter—a *lot* of glitter. When the unicorn shook itself dry after its daily glitter bath (the same way a dog does), the entire house became coated in layers and layers of sparkly stuff as far as the eye could see.

And the thing about glitter? You can *never* get rid of it once it's in your house. Isabella's dad was *not* happy. "I can't go to work like this! My suit is coated in glitter! I look like a crafts project, not a lawyer!"

On the plus side, the unicorn did not make normal poop—*it pooped rainbows*. The colorful poop smelled like strawberry-watermelon candy, which made cleaning up sort of fun. There was never a question as to where the unicorn pooped—anyone could see the glowing rainbow pile anywhere in the house.

Stepped in poop? No problem! You're walking on rainbows the rest of the day!

That's how Isabella thought about it. Her parents—not so much.

It took a week for Isabella's parents to finally accept the unicorn as part of the family. It caused tens of thousands of dollars in property damage and ate the family goldfish. But, hey, it made Isabella happy. So her parents said she could keep it—chained and collared outside.

When Isabella was about to put the collar around the unicorn's neck, it grew wings and flew away. Unicorns are like that.

CHAPTER 4
Benji

Benji couldn't believe Isabella asked for a unicorn. That was gonna be *his* wish! He wasn't going to be a total dork and ask the ~~genie~~ djinn for the same thing. He wanted to do something original. But Benji had to rethink his wish and *fast*. After all, he was next in line.

"*Ahem*," the djinn said, growing impatient with Benji. "Are you going to make a wish or not, little man?"

"Yes!" Benji said, still thinking. "I wish for... I wish for...I wish for..."

The djinn rolled his eyes. "I wish you'd hurry up—"

Benji panicked and blurted out: "...A DINOSAUR!"

"Wish granted!" the djinn said.

Taking care of a fully grown dinosaur is a lot different than caring for a new puppy or kitten or sugar glider. For starters, those animals can all fit neatly inside a shoe box. The *T. rex* was bigger than Benji's whole bedroom. So Rexy—as Benji soon named his female dino pet—stayed in the backyard.

You can imagine the neighbors' shock when they came out to water their lawn the next day. Benji's mom heard their screams and told Benji his "pet" was chasing a crowd of people down the street.

"Oops!" Benji said. "I'm sure Rexy's just chasing them with her sharp teeth in a *friendly* way. I play with my friends like that all the time."

Benji bared his teeth and pretended to stalk his mom around the kitchen. She wasn't buying it. "Train her better or she's going right back to your school, bubee."

Another difference between dinos and other pets is how they play with their owners. New kittens and parakeets form a bond with their human owners. They like that they look different. But not dinosaurs...

Any creature that wasn't another dinosaur drove Rexy into a crazed, hangry rage. Mail carriers, small animals, airplanes, you name it. Birds refused to fly over the neighborhood now— Rexy had eaten too many of them. Benji almost lost his arm the first time he tried to feed her.

"Why does Rexy have to eat *everything*?!" Benji wondered aloud.

"She's just lonely," Benji's dad said from the living room. "All her friends are dead. So she's eating her feelings."

Benji came up with an idea.

He left Rexy to chase squirrels (and a few cars) while he went to the Halloween store. "Do you have any dinosaur costumes?" he asked.

A few minutes later, Rexy stopped roaring at clouds long enough to notice another dinosaur walking up. It was teensy, but it had *Stegosaurus* plates and a spiked tail. It also wore a yarmulke. It was a *Benji-saurus*.

Rexy let out a little yip and a roar. Rexy was finally happy—she had a dinosaur playmate.

Together, *Benji-saurus* and Rexy took long walks along the beach and swam in the ocean. They played fetch, dug up yards for bones, and played hide-and-seek in the woods. (Let me tell you: Campers did not like that one.)

Benji-saurus and Rexy were great—when it

was just the two of them. Anytime other people showed up, Rexy got hangry again. Like when Benji invited Liam and Fatima over to show off his dinosaur. The moment Rexy roared, they screamed at the top of their lungs, sprinting away and waving their arms around like crazy people. Big mistake!

Rexy demolished half the neighborhood chasing after them.

Benji's mom was there to give him another warning. "Liam's parents are threatening to sue us. Get your dinosaur under control! And no dessert tonight, bubee, for either of you!"

Benji-saurus went to bed hungry that night. And so did Rexy.

"Why do you keep doing this, Rexy?" Benji asked from his window. As he stared out at the sleeping dinosaur in his backyard, he noticed his neighbor taking out the trash. Mr. Sheezenstein was his name, and he was a weirdly shaped man—he was orange from spray tan and had a square body with tiny little legs. Benji used to joke with his dad that Mr. Sheezenstein looked like a cheese cube with legs.

Mr. CHEESE-en-stein they called him (though not to his face).

Same for Liam and that dumb sweat suit he wore the other day when he came over. It was yellow sweats and a T-shirt with pepperonis all over. Liam called it his "little *slice* of cool." Everyone in class joked that it made Liam look like a walking pizza.

And that's when it dawned on Benji.

"We look like food to Rexy. That's why she's chasing us!" Benji realized.

The next day, Benji made bright neon flyers and tacked them up all over the neighborhood. Under a picture of Rexy, the flyer read:

HAVE YOU SEEN THIS DINO?

WELL, SHE'S SEEN YOU!
AND YOU LOOK LIKE FOOD TO HER!

PLEASE DO NOT WEAR ANY FOOD-THEMED CLOTHING.
(This means you, Liam.)

DO NOT BARBECUE.
(This makes you smell like hot dogs and hamburgers.)

AND DO NOT WEAR DEODORANT.
(If you smell good, she might think you taste good.)

PLEASE FOLLOW THESE SIMPLE RULES:
<u>DON'T</u> DRESS LIKE FOOD.
<u>DON'T</u> SMELL LIKE FOOD.
JUST SMELL BAD,
AND YOU'RE ALL GOOD!

Thanks,
Benji (your neighbor)

People listened and things calmed down after that. That was, until a new food truck came to town. It was shaped like a giant hot dog on wheels. As soon as Rexy saw it, she had to devour it. She chased that food truck down the highway and right out of town. Benji never saw Rexy again, but he hoped that—wherever she was— she was happy.

CHAPTER 5
Zoey

Zoey was the shortest girl in Classroom 13. How short? Well, she could wear her mom's high heels, gel her hair straight up like she'd stuck her finger in an electrical socket, stand on three or four phone books, and *still* not be as tall as Mark.

Zoey hated being short.

She wanted to get a good look at the strange

blue man, but she couldn't quite see over Benji's head. She strained, getting on her tippy-toes.

Still, no luck.

She needed to be taller. She'd always thought life would be better if she were taller: If she were, she could see over people's heads in a crowd and in movie theaters. She could finally reach the good pudding her father stashed in the high kitchen cabinet (which he never shared). And best of all, she could fulfill her dream of becoming a supermodel.

Zoey wanted to be tall and glamorous like the women in her mom's fashion magazines. And the ~~genie~~ djinn could make it happen.

When it was her turn, Zoey said, "I wish to be *taller!*"

"Wish granted, short stack!" the djinn said.

As the magic swirled all around her in a mini cyclone, Zoey could feel herself *growing*. Her fingers felt like they were stretching out of her hands. Her legs lifted her body up like she was on an elevator. And as the gold dust settled, her head bumped into the ceiling!

Zoey was now twelve feet tall.

The whole class gasped. "How's the view up there?" Liam asked. "Can you see the spitball I launched earlier?"

It was right next to her head. She could see it. It was gross. And she couldn't have been happier.

But being twelve feet tall was not as fun as Zoey thought it would be.

For starters, she could see above the heads of any crowd. But everyone stared at her. And in the movie theater, anyone sitting behind her shouted, "I can't see over your big head!"

Zoey thought some of her dad's good pudding would make her feel better. She went to the kitchen, excited to raid his hidden stash. But when she got there, she found she couldn't even squeeze into the kitchen. She was too tall.

If that wasn't bad enough, none of Zoey's clothes fit anymore. Her mom had spent a fortune buying her fancy clothes. Now they had to sew all her clothes together to make Zoey one big dress. It did *not* look pretty.

Zoey cried and cried. (And her dad *still* wouldn't share his pudding. It was almost dinnertime. He didn't want her to ruin her appetite.)

But it wasn't all bad news. The local basketball team asked her to try out. Zoey did, and she was quite good.

CHAPTER 6
William

When William woke up that morning, he didn't feel like going to school. Since his parents had run off with his fortune, he lived with his grandparents now. And they were extremely gullible. So when he told them he had a terrible stomachache, they let him stay home.

His grandma made him drink some pink liquid that tasted like chalk. As she and Grandpa

left for a day of shuffleboard and Jell-O eating with friends, she said, "Call us if you need anything."

As soon as the door closed, William hopped up and did his happy dance. He did *not* have a stomachache. He turned on the TV and found a cartoon marathon. Then he started eating all the junk food in the house. By his fourth bag of chips and eighth soda and third bag of candy and second microwave pizza, he *did* have a stomachache.

He felt awful—so awful, in fact, that he puked all over himself and the TV.

TVs are not designed to withstand vomit, so it broke. His grandparents made him stay home from school for the rest of the week so they could "watch over him and nurse him back to health." That meant he didn't get to watch any cartoons.

The worst part is that he would feel even

more awful once he discovered he'd missed out on the chance to make any wish he wanted. He could have wished to never go to school again. Too bad he wasn't at school to make that wish.

CHAPTER 7
Mark

Mark—now the *second*-tallest student in Classroom 13 (after Zoey)—was very handsome. All the girls had a crush on him. But he only had eyes for one woman—Lynda Carter, an actress who once played the superhero Wonder Woman. One of the things he loved about Wonder Woman was that she flew in an invisible plane. Mark wanted to fly, too.

During class, Mark often daydreamed about what it would be like to fly above the clouds. He imagined waving at his friends from above the trees and taking naps among the birds. He wanted to zoom around the world and visit strange places.

Sometimes, he jumped off the stairs in his house just to see if he could fly. (He couldn't.)

So when the ~~genie~~ djinn came to Classroom 13 and said he would grant everyone one wish, Mark knew exactly what he would wish for. When it was finally his turn, Mark walked up to the ghostly blue wish-maker and said, "I wish I could fly."

The djinn turned him into a duck.

Now that Mark was a mallard (that's a kind of duck), Mark forgot that he was previously a human boy. He flapped his wings, took off clumsily, and flew out the window. He had to hurry if he wanted to join the other birds as they went north for the winter. Or did birds go south for the summer? Or was it west for spring break? He couldn't remember. So he just flew.

Mark ate live insects when he was hungry and pooped wherever he wanted. (Mostly on cars and on people, because even as a duck, he thought that was funny.) Though he couldn't remember Lynda Carter or being a student in Classroom 13, he *did* know that he was very happy when he was flying.

As Classroom 13's resident do-gooder, Chloe felt it was her duty to give her wish away. And why not? She spent all the other days of the year giving all sorts of stuff away to people or organizations that needed it more than her.

She gave canned goods to the hungry.

She donated clothes to the needy.

She mailed seeds to the seedless.

She even gifted gummy bears to the gummy-bear-less!

Chloe *cared*.

"Can I give my wish to someone else?" Chloe asked the ~~genie~~ djinn.

"Why?" the djinn asked, concerned. "No one gives away their wish. Is this a trick? Are you trying to use your wish for evil? Granting evil wishes makes me feel really crummy about my line of work."

"No!" Chloe said. "Nothing like that at all. I want to give my wish away to someone in need. It's kind of my thing."

The djinn shrugged. "Very well. Let's have it, then. Just say the words."

"I wish to give my wish away to someone else, somewhere far away, who really needs it and deserves it."

At that exact moment, on the other side of the world, a young girl named Tanvi said: "I wish I had a dragon."

And *POOF!* An enormous fire-breathing dragon appeared out of thin air. Tanvi could barely believe it—a real live dragon! And it was all *hers!*

The little girl ran outside with a big smile on her face to greet her new friend.

"My name is Tanvi," the little girl said. "What's yours?"

But you see, dragons don't speak any human languages. So to him, the little girl may as well have said: "Hello, Mr. Dragon, I hope you're hungry because I'd make a great after-dinner snack."

And she did. The dragon gobbled her up.

"That was a very generous thing you did," Ms. Linda said.

"Thanks," Chloe said with a smile, imagining all the good she'd done with her wish. She returned to her seat, happy to have helped someone.

CHAPTER 9
Santiago

Santiago's mom made him stay home. That's why he didn't get a wish from the Grand Djinn that day. Last time this happened, he vowed to never miss school again. Of course, as you probably know, life rarely goes according to plan. Especially where moms are concerned. Moms always get their way.

CHAPTER 10
Dev

Dev was Classroom 13's biggest gamer. Sure, other kids played games here and there, but not like Dev. He was competitive about it. For him, games were a way of life.

If it took him a whole week without sleep to beat a game, he'd do it. If discovering every hidden power-up and gem in a level meant missing his favorite TV show, so be it. He didn't care about skipping family dinners or pizza parties—those were distractions without a pause button.

Video games were the only thing that mattered.

So you can only imagine how painful *losing* a game was to Dev. And that's exactly why he'd been so moody lately. A friend of the family (who was a video game designer) gave Dev the chance to play a new game before anyone else. It was called *Teddy Bear Bashers: Space Capades*.

Dev thought he'd beat it in a week.

Instead, he was going on four and a half weeks of losing on the same exact level, over and over and over.

Dev hadn't slept. He'd barely eaten. And he smelled. Who had time for baths when ultimate teddy-bear-bashing victory was on the line?

Not Dev. He was a teddy-bear-bashing space ace. But he needed to know how to beat the final boss. How were you supposed to bash the armada of alien-teddy-bear spaceships? There were millions of them! And when you bashed one, two more took its place. It was impossible.

When it was Dev's turn to make a wish, he said, "Yo, Djinn! How do I beat the final level of *Teddy Bear Bashers: Space Capades?*"

"That's your wish?"

Dev shook his head wildly.

"Easy," the djinn said. "Don't bash."

"*Don't* bash?" Dev said. "But it's called *Teddy Bear Bashers.*"

"If you don't bash, the enemy armada doesn't know you're there. You press up, float to the top of the screen for a little while, fly over them, and, *badda bing, badda boom*, you're at the end of the level. Game over."

Dev couldn't believe it. It was that easy? *Don't bash?!*

"But...but..."

"No buts, no nuts, no coconuts. That's game over," the djinn said. "Next!"

CHAPTER 11
Yuna

The ~~genie~~ djinn let out a long, heavy sigh, then cracked his knuckles. He was clearly annoyed.

"What's wrong?" Ms. Linda asked. "Are you still thirsty? Those juice boxes *are* rather small. Would you like something else? Lamp oil? Lamp oil with ice?"

The Grand Djinn cleared his throat. "If granting wishes for your class wasn't strange enough, this girl won't even tell me what her wish is," the blue man replied. "She keeps passing me notes that make no sense."

"Oh, you must be talking about Yuna," Ms. Linda said. "She's a mystery."

The only thing Yuna's classmates and teacher knew about her was...well, nothing. She never said a word, choosing instead to communicate only in code, like a spy. Too bad the ~~genie~~ djinn and Ms. Linda couldn't figure it out.

Here's what her note said:

I WISH FOR A SUPER-SECRET SPY MISSION. SO SECRET THAT NO ONE KNOWS ABOUT IT. NOT EVEN ME.

CHAPTER 12
Liam

Liam wasn't one to brag, but he'd accomplished a lot for a boy his age. He was undefeated in the Classroom 13 prank wars. He was one of the youngest *Global Book of World Records* record holders (for Most Powerful Fart Ever Farted by a Human Being). And just this morning, he'd had the most brilliant idea known to mankind.

Well, *mer*mankind...

"I'm going to learn how to breathe under-water for a really long time," he told his friends at the bus stop before school. "That way I can be a merman."

"Why do you want to be a merman?" Dev asked.

"Have you *seen* mermaids? They're beautiful! Plus, all mermen have perfect abs. I wouldn't even have to do sit-ups. I could just watch monster movies all day and have abs. My idea is *ABS*-so-lutely genius!"

Liam laughed and laughed at that. Dev just shook his head.

"*ABS*-so-lutely!" Liam repeated over and over. He chuckled at his own cleverness. No one found Liam's jokes funnier than Liam himself. The entire way to school that morning, it was all Liam could think about.

Liam had no idea how to learn to hold his breath underwater. But once Ms. Linda freed that ~~genie~~ djinn, he knew his wish.

*   *   *

Having seen a few kids' wishes backfire already, Liam should've known to choose his words carefully. It was all about phrasing with this fussy blue wish-granter. But Liam was too focused on holding in a big fart. (If he held them in, they just got bigger, which he thought was funny.)

"I wish I could breathe underwater!" Liam said.

The Grand Djinn didn't even bother to look up at him. He conjured a magical cloud out of thin air for the boy and *poof*!

Suddenly, Liam felt light-headed. His heart began to race. The world went all blurry. He felt like he couldn't breathe—probably because he couldn't.

Liam had wished to breathe underwater. He hadn't said anything about still being able to breathe air. The djinn had given him gills.

175

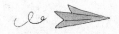

Like a fish on dry land, Liam was flailing all around, gasping for help. He needed to be submerged in water to breathe.

Luckily, Olivia—the smartest girl in Classroom 13—spotted the gills. "He needs water!" She grabbed the class fishbowl and shoved it (upside down) onto his head.

The students and teacher of Classroom 13 waited, hoping for the best....

A few seconds later, Liam opened his eyes and saw his classmates looking back at him. He smiled and waved.

"Hey, it worked! I can breathe underwater," Liam said—though no one could understand him. (Have you ever tried having a conversation underwater? It's impossible to hear anything. It just sounds like mumbles and bubbles.)

"What did he say?" Teo asked.

"Je pense qu'il a dit qu'il est comme un homme-poisson," Hugo said.

While the rest of Classroom 13 resumed their places in line for the djinn, Liam checked for the abs. He lifted his shirt and found his same old tummy.

But Liam didn't mind. Life underwater was better than abs. His fishbowl magnified everything, so real life looked way more 3-D than usual. Bonus! And Olivia didn't bother to empty the fish from the fishbowl before she shoved it onto his head. Two little goldfish swam around his face. New underwater best buds. Double bonus!

"Hello, little fish friends," Liam said, bubbles floating up on every word. "I am your new aquatic overlord. You may call me Liam the Merman! No, Aqua King! No, wait...just Liam!"

He may not have been given the abs, or a fishtail, or a magical trident, but Liam felt like a true merman. He relaxed and began to enjoy his new life "under the sea."

Having spent his wish, Ms. Linda asked him to return to his desk. Liam decided that his first act as Classroom 13's resident merman would be to finally let his fart out. (He'd been saving it up all morning.) He discovered that the fishbowl made an airtight seal around his neck, so he couldn't smell it. Triple bonus!

But everyone else could smell it. It smelled like dead fish. Everyone gagged.

"How *fart*-tastic was that?" Liam said, laughing. "Enjoy, landlubbers."

CHAPTER 13

The 13th Classroom

Classroom 13 didn't get a wish. It tried to speak up and say it wanted a wish, but the ~~genie~~ djinn and the students couldn't hear the Classroom. (As you may or may not know, 13th Classrooms are *very* quiet speakers. Mostly they just whisper.)

Filled with rage at being forgotten once again, the 13th Classroom vowed revenge (for the second time) on all of Ms. Linda's students....

CHAPTER 14
Ava

Ava is one of those rare people who is good at many things. She is beautiful, smart, and a wonderful friend. But sometimes, she was too smart for her own good. For instance, on the day the ~~genie~~ djinn came to Classroom 13, Ava was feeling particularly cunning. When the djinn said every student could have *one* wish, she knew exactly what her wish would be...

...to have *more* wishes, of course!

When it was her turn, she walked up to the djinn with her hands on her hips and a sly smile on her face. Bored of granting wishes, the djinn was picking at his fingernails. "What's your wish? Let me guess, you want a pony or superpowers?"

"No. I want something better. I wish..." Ava said, pausing for dramatic effect, "...for *unlimited* wishes."

The djinn sat up straight and smiled. "You do?"

"It's a no-brainer!" Ava said.

The rest of the students in Classroom 13 groaned. That was a great wish. They should have thought of that.

"Are you absolutely, positively certain that's what you want your wish to be?" the djinn said, as if trying to hide his excitement. This was kind of a weird reaction, but it didn't stop Ava.

"I am absolutely, positively certain that's what I want my wish to be," Ava said.

"Then say it one more time," the djinn said.

"I wish for *unlimited* wishes."

"Wish granted!" the djinn said, snapping his fingers. Gold magic and purple smoke swirled around Ava. A moment later, she turned into a ghostly blue girl and got sucked into her own golden lamp.

"What did you do?!" Ava cried, banging on the lamp to escape.

"I granted your wish and made you a djinn," the djinn explained. "You see, the only person who can have *unlimited* wishes is a djinn. Of course, a djinn doesn't get to wish anything for his- or herself. But they *do* have an unlimited amount of wishes to grant for others. You're welcome."

CHAPTER 15
Teo

Teo immediately grabbed the new golden lamp and rubbed it. The new ~~genie~~ djinn Ava popped out of the lamp in a *poof* of magic and smoke. "What do you want?" she yelled.

"I want my wish," Teo said.

"No," Ava said. "I don't want to be a djinn. I'm not granting any wishes."

"But you have to!" Teo said.

"No, I don't," Ava said, going back into her lamp. Teo rubbed the lamp again, and Ava popped out again. "Stop that!"

"Not until you grant my wish!"

"You're as annoying as a little brother," Ava said.

"And you're as annoying as an older sister," Teo said. "But you still have to grant my wish!"

Ava looked at the Grand Djinn. He nodded. "It's true. This is your new job now. You're the one who asked for unlimited wishes. Well, now you have them—for other people."

"Ugh!" Ava grumped. "Fine. What's your wish, Teo?"

"I wish to be the richest person in the world!" Like Ava, Teo was also quite smart. But he should have paid better attention to how Ava's wish backfired. He should have made certain to think of his wish phrasing perfectly.

Ava got a sly look on her face and winked at

the djinn. They both giggled. "Oh. That's an easy wish." She snapped her fingers.

Teo waited. He expected his wallet to explode with cash, or his clothes to turn into solid gold, or a chauffeur to drive up in a limo and drive him to a mansion. But none of those things happened. "Where's my money?!" Teo whined.

"You didn't say anything about money," Ava said, still giggling.

"Did you muck up my wish?" Teo growled.

"Not at all," Ava said. "You said you wanted to be rich. You didn't realize it, but you were *already* the richest person in the world—rich in *love*, from your family."

His parents and grandparents and uncles and aunts and cousins ran into the room and started hugging him and kissing him and telling him how much they loved him.

Teo pulled his hair and screamed. "I wasted my wish!"

"No takesies backsies," Ava said. She and the Grand Djinn exchanged a fist bump.

"You're going to make an excellent djinn, young lady," the Grand Djinn said.

"Thank you." Ava smiled.

CHAPTER 16
Jayden Jason

After Teo threw a tantrum about how bad his wish turned out and how it was "totally Ava's fault," Jayden Jason James (Triple J for short) wasn't taking any chances. He rubbed the Grand Djinn's lamp instead.

The sour blue man reappeared in a huff. "I'm on break! Take your wishes to my apprentice."

"Yeah, about that—we took a vote, and the class agrees we would rather *you* handle the wishes from now on," Triple J explained. "Since you're more experienced and all. No offense, Ava."

"None taken!" Ava shouted. She stuck her tongue out at Teo and squeezed back into her lamp.

"What'll it be, kid?" the Grand Djinn asked.

Triple J took a long, deep breath. The rest of Classroom 13 was on pins and needles. They knew he would do something cool with his wish. Triple J was the most popular kid in school. The class couldn't wait to hear what ~~their~~ his wish would be.

"I wish every day was a snow day!" Triple J said.

The whole class erupted into applause. Infinite snow days?! They'd never have to come to school again! It was genius! They hoisted Triple J up on their shoulders, parading him around the room like the town hero, chanting, *"Tri-ple J! Tri-ple J! Tri-ple J!"*

Suddenly, a chill came over the room. The kids could see their breath! They ran to the windows. Outside, all they could see was white in every direction. The town was invisible, blanketed in the thickest snow they'd ever seen.

Ms. Linda turned on the news on the class TV just as a reporter said: "The National Weather Service is calling this one *Super Snow-zilla Ice-pocalypse Freeze-mageddon*—the winter storm to end all winter storms. The forecast calls for nonstop blizzards forever...and ever...*and ever*! If you go outside, you're likely to freeze instantly. That means, wherever you are, stay put."

Everyone's jaw dropped. They were snowed in—*at school*!

The Grand Djinn giggled, *poof*ing himself up a huge winter coat and a hot cocoa. "Ta-ta, kids! Enjoy the snow. I'll be in my lamp!"

In a flash of sparkles, he was gone. And so was the happy chanting for Triple J.

CHAPTER 17
Sophia

Being snowed in at school was *not* the winter wonderland Triple J had in mind when he'd made his wish. Everyone huddled together, teeth chattering, trying to stay warm.

The door to Classroom 13 opened, letting in a cold draft. Ms. Linda slammed it back shut, having returned from her pilgrimage to the school gymnasium. The unlucky teacher looked like she'd just returned from hiking Mount Everest. "I borrowed the gym parachute. Every-one crawl beneath it. Our combined body heat will help keep us warm.

"Okay, everyone in?" the teacher asked. "Olivia and Liam, this is your cue."

Olivia reluctantly pulled Liam's finger. He let out a dangerously large fart. It smelled like rotten eggs, but the gas blast was warm enough to heat the whole parachute in seconds. The kids held their noses as they warmed up.

"Whose turn is it to make their wish?" Ms. Linda asked.

It was Sophia's turn. But her hearing aids had frozen and she couldn't hear anything. It didn't matter to her. While the students worried about themselves, Sophia was more worried about the plants outside.

Sophia went to the window and saw the Classroom 13 garden covered in snow and ice.

"Oh no! The plants!"

She ran to the djinn lamp, rubbed it furiously until he came out, and said, "I wish to undo Triple J's wish."

"Done," the djinn said, snapping his fingers.

The blizzard vanished, and the plants were blooming in the sunshine. "Whew," Sophia said, relieved.

"Good job!" Ms. Linda said. "You saved the class from freezing!"

All the students hugged Sophia and patted her on the back. Her hearing aids began to thaw, just in time for Chloe to say, "I'm surprised at how you spent your wish. I thought for sure you'd use your wish to make the world a more eco-friendly place."

Sophia looked outside at the classroom garden, then thought of *all* the plants in the whole wide world.

For the rest of the day, Sophia couldn't help but wonder if she'd made a terrible mistake....

CHAPTER 18
Earl

Earl had no idea what was going on. Probably because he was a hamster, which meant he was neither excited nor unexcited to meet the djinn. As long as the djinn didn't tap on the glass of his tank like the students in Classroom 13, Earl honestly didn't care.

But when the students insisted that the hamster get a wish, the ghostly blue man shrugged and said, "Sure, why not?"

The djinn turned to the hamster and said, "You get one wish, Earl. What will it be?"

At that moment, all Earl was thinking about was sunflower seeds. So when he squeaked (in his native language of Hamsterish), he said, "I wish for sunflower seeds."

His tank was filled to brimming with sunflower seeds. Earl was very happy. If only everyone could think like Earl.

CHAPTER 19
Lily

Lily Lin was the youngest of five children in her family, and she was the only girl. This meant she had to deal with four annoying older brothers. They loved Lily, but they were only nice to her on holidays. The rest of the year, they teased her. This involved tying her shoelaces together, pulling her hair, or jumping out from behind doors and scaring her.

As it always is for the youngest kid, life at

home was no picnic for Lily Lin. But you'd never know that by talking to her.

Lily was outgoing and bold but could be quite intense. For example, during her book report on *Charlotte's Web*, she concluded that it was "unrealistic that a spider and a pig would become friends." (Ms. Linda gave her a B- and encouraged her to have a more open mind. Lily protested until Ms. Linda gave her an A.)

Today, with an opportunity to have any wish, Lily knew what she wanted—an edge over her older, stronger brothers.

Lily approached the djinn and said, "I want to be stronger."

The djinn stared at her.

"Please," Lily added.

"You must use the words 'I wish,'" the djinn explained.

"I wish."

"Now put that all together in one sentence."

"Oh. I wish to have lots and lots of muscles."

But the Grand Djinn must have had lamp oil clogging his ears because he heard Lily say "mussels." Which, though the two words sound the same, are very different.

Muscles are tissues of the body that contract to produce motion. They make people fast and strong.

Mussels are bivalve mollusks, similar to clams, that people like to eat in their seafood medley, along with other weird things that have tentacles. (Gross, right?)

With a snap of the djinn's fingers, *mussels* rained down all over Lily. She was very confused. So were the other kids.

"As the only merman in this class, this offends me!" Liam said. Though no one could understand his bubbling mumbling through the fishbowl.

Lily picked up one of the mussels and sniffed it. The salty ocean smell reminded her why her family *never* ate seafood. Gathering up the mussels, Lily stuffed them into her backpack. She walked home with a smile on her face.

Opening her backpack, the smell of the salty shellfish warmed Lily's heart. She put the mussels all around her room, rubbed them on her shoelaces, and washed her hair with them.

When her brothers got home, they went to pull her hair. But before they could touch her, she said, "Shellfish."

They froze. When they sniffed the air, they all recoiled in fear.

"We're *allergic* to shellfish!" her brothers cried. If they ate or touched shellfish, their hands would blow up like balloons, and they'd have to be rushed to the hospital.

"Then it would be best to leave me alone," Lily said. "No more teasing."

Lily was now untouchable.

She bossed her brothers around and made them wait on her hand and foot like servants. If they started to be bratty, she'd reach out as if she were going to touch them and say, "Shellfish." They'd return to being on their best behavior for her.

Sure, Lily smelled like old seafood all the time now, but it was totally worth it.

CHAPTER 20
Mason

Ask anyone in Classroom 13 about Mason, and they'll tell you he's nice, funny, great at soccer, and really strong. The one thing they won't say is that he's smart.

Because he's not.

Mason didn't understand basic math, was a horrible speller, and still thought Christopher Columbus was the first basketball player to ever walk on the moon.

(Hint: He wasn't.)

Mason could've asked the ~~genie~~ djinn for a high IQ or wished to have the best grades in school. He could've even wished to never have to do homework again. He could've wished to be transformed into a super-smart, super-strong soccer-playing machine. He could have wished for anything. The sky was the limit.

Instead Mason wished for a flashlight.

As I mentioned, he's *not* the smartest kid....

The Grand Djinn just sat there, stupefied. "Kiddo, you *are* aware I am the great and powerful djinn. Sultans have asked me for fortunes and superpowers and all manner of things beyond imagination. I've given blind men their sight back and turned whole cities into dust. And here you are, asking me for a... *flashlight?*"

"Yeah!" Mason said, totally happy with his wish. "I wish for a flashlight. But a really good one!"

The blue wish-maker twirled his pinkie and—*poof!*—a brand-new flashlight appeared in Mason's hands. It still had the price tag on it: $14.99 with tax. Available at any store.

"Woo-hoo!" Mason yelled.

That day, he went home and used his new flashlight to make shadow puppets on the wall. Then he went downstairs into his scary basement and chased all the spiders away by shining his light in every nook and cranny. After that, he pointed it at his own face, under his chin, to make funny-creepy faces to scare his mom when she least expected it.

"OoooohOhhhhOhhh!" Mason said, trying to sound like a ghost. "I'm here to haunt yooooOOUUUUUuuuu...."

"Mason, go away. I'm trying to brush my teeth," his mom said, a white ring of toothpaste around her mouth.

Mason turned the flashlight off. "It's me, Mom. It's Mason. Bet you thought I was a ghost, thanks to my handy-dandy flashlight! Guess what I named him."

"Who?"

"The flashlight!"

"You named your flashlight?"

"His name is Mortimer!"

"That's nice, dear," his mom said, going back to brushing her teeth. She shut the bathroom door.

Mason took Mortimer the Flashlight everywhere. Thanks to its always-bright shine, Mason was now the *brightest* kid in school.

But he still wasn't smart.

CHAPTER 21
Hugo

*H*ugo avait hâte que ce soit son tour. Il savait déjà exactement ce qu'il allait demander. Malheureusement, il était le dernier de la file.

Pendant que les autres élèves faisaient leurs vœux, Hugo s'impatientait de plus en plus. "J'en ai assez d'attendre," dit-il à haute voix. "Je voudrais être le premier en ligne."

Le génie l'entendit et dit, "Vœu exaucé!"

Hugo disparut, puis réapparut à l'avant de la file. Il fit un grand sourire et dit, "C'est mon tour maintenant!"

"Désolé, gamin," dit le génie. "Un seul souhait par personne. C'est comme ça. Au suivant!"

CHAPTER 22

Emma

Emma Embry stepped up to make her wish but walked right past the Grand Djinn. She rubbed Ava's lamp instead.

Ava appeared, very surprised to be summoned, in a *poof*! "Did you rub my lamp by accident?" she asked.

"No, my wish is kind of a personal one," Emma whispered. "And if I have to ask a blue person to help me with it, I'd rather it be a blue person I know. No offense, Mr. Genie."

"It's DJINN!" the Grand Djinn shouted. Before his head fully disappeared back under, he added, "Don't come complaining to me if she whiffs on your wish. Silly girl!"

"I won't whiff," Ava assured Emma.

"It's about my parents," Emma said. "I wish they were...*un*-divorced."

The whole class reacted with a loud gasp. Everyone knew Emma's parents (the town's premier interior decorators), but no one knew they'd gotten divorced.

"I just saw your parents together the other day," Olivia said, confused.

"They still *work* together, but they don't live together," Emma explained. "I've been spending the week with Mom at our house and the weekends with Dad at his new apartment. I hate it."

"But isn't your dad's new place nice?" asked Isabella.

"Of course it's beautiful," Emma said. "He's a decorator. But his new place is so small. It doesn't have a lot of room to sit and cry, or lie down and wallow in despair, or walk comfortably while arguing with the divorce lawyer about what *I* want."

"That sounds awful," Benji said. A lot of the kids in the 13th Classroom gave Emma a hug.

"Let's get this fixed," Ava said. "I hereby pronounce your wish *GRANTED*. I hereby pronounce your mom and dad *husband and wife*. Again."

After school, Emma ran home to find her mom and dad together again, side by side, in the kitchen. They were even holding hands.

Emma was so happy she felt like crying. "Mom, Dad, you guys are—"

"Miserable!" her mom said.

"Honey, you don't know where Daddy's handsaw is, do you? It wasn't in the rustic Victorian steamer trunk where I usually store it," her dad said.

"Why do you need a handsaw?" Emma asked. As she got within hugging distance of her parents, she realized they weren't holding hands—they were shackled to each other by a pair of enchanted handcuffs.

"We tried gardening shears, but they weren't strong enough to cut through these chains. Just like *I told you*," her mom snapped at her dad.

"Oh, well, *excuuuuuse* me for coming up with a logical solution to our illogical handcuff problem!" her dad snapped back.

And just like that, they were arguing about how to cut off the handcuffs. Emma did her best to ignore the shouting and hug them. "Mom, Dad, please stop fighting!"

They tried to, for Emma's sake. But it didn't

last. During dinner, they were at it again. Mom wanted to use her right arm to reach for veggies, while Dad was trying to spoon some mashed potatoes with his left. Handcuffs made eating very difficult. No one got what they wanted, so Emma's mom and dad went back for a second helping—of their argument.

Emma took turns feeding them.

"Sorry, honey," her dad said, chewing a mouthful of mashed potatoes. "Please know this has nothing to do with you."

"I'm sorry, too," her mom added, chomping down on asparagus. "I'm extra sorry."

"Well, I'm way *more* sorry than you are!" her dad yelled. And then they were fighting again.

It was becoming clear to Emma that maybe her parents *shouldn't* be back together.

The next day, Emma decided to help them. She asked their handyman neighbor to cut through the handcuffs with his chain saw. But it was no use. The cuffs were too strong for normal power tools.

"This is hopeless," her dad said.

"Being married to you is hopeless," her mom added.

Emma called a cab, and the three of them rode to a local power plant with a billboard on the outside that promised THE WORLD'S MOST POWERFUL ATOMIC LASER—AND GIFT SHOP! Her mom and dad paid the laser operator two hundred bucks to zap the cuffs off. All the laser did was heat the chains up until they glowed red.

Not even the world's most powerful atomic laser was powerful enough to cut through the djinn magic. Emma's parents survived the laser blast, but all they got was a lousy T-shirt and some minor wrist burns.

Emma's parents argued in the backseat of the cab the entire way to the diamond-cutting facility on the other side of town. Emma struggled to hear the diamond cutter over her parents' bickering. "This is not a normal drill bit," the diamond cutter said. "This will cut through diamond. This will cut anything."

But the diamond-cutting drill bit was no match for the enchanted handcuffs, either. Emma's parents went back to fighting.

"My parents were the same way," the diamond cutter told Emma. "They were much happier *after* they separated."

Emma knew the diamond cutter was right. Her parents were happier apart. She had to let go.

Emma had no idea how she was going to fix this. But she had an idea to get them to stop fighting. The cab stopped at her parents' furniture warehouse. She found two antique room dividers and brought them home. These were the kind of little walls that could be folded up and put anywhere. Movie stars used them to get dressed while other people were in the same room. But Emma had a better use for it.

At home, she unfolded the room dividers, putting them between her mom and her dad. They didn't have to see each other (except through the crack where their hands were linked), which meant they didn't fight (as much). And Emma still got to have both her parents in the same house.

She took turns feeding them mashed potatoes and asparagus. It was exhausting, but it seemed to be working fine for now. There was just one problem—what was going to happen when they had to go to the bathroom?

CHAPTER 23
Fatima

If you took a poll and asked everyone in Classroom 13 what they thought Fatima would wish for, you'd probably hear them say:

"Comic books!"

"Comics, definitely."

"I bet she asks for every comic book issue ever made."

"What he said. Comics."

"Probably every single number one issue that's ever come out—bagged and boarded, of course."

"An ant farm!" (This last one was Mason's guess. He was wrong.)

Yes, Fatima was Classroom 13's avid comic-book collector. And her wish did have something to do with comics but not how you might think.

"I wish to live inside a comic book," Fatima told the Grand Djinn.

"Done!" the djinn said as a magic tornado of gold dust whisked her away into the black-and-white pages of a comic-book world.

"Black-and-white?!" Fatima whined. "This isn't the comic I meant...."

Fatima didn't recognize her new surroundings at all. The art style looked so normal and boring, like old drawings of a normal and boring neighborhood.

Where were the wizards? Where were the

alien galaxies? Where were the superpowers and the supervillains? Where was the action?!

"Welcome!" said a cartoon boy with a round, chubby face.

Fatima noticed "Welcome!" appeared above him in a *speech bubble*—a floating cloud in comics that spelled out everything a character said.

Fatima looked at her hands. They were cartoony, too: curved and with only four fingers. She didn't care that she was missing a finger, but seriously, where was her superhero costume? Where was her laser gun?

"What kind of comic *is* this?!" Fatima asked.

"The best comic strip in the newspaper, of course: *Silly Willy!*"

The harsh truth dawned on Fatima. She wasn't in one of her favorite comic *books*, she was in a comic *strip*. Didn't a djinn know the difference? (Probably not. Comic books are relatively new compared to ancient mystical wish-granters.) And worse, it was the same lame comic strip old people used to giggle at in the Sunday newspaper.

In this comic, there were no robots or dragons or mutants or ninja assassins. There were no superheroes or cyborgs or vampires or werewolves or transforming machines from another world. There were no cryoprisons or black holes or spaceships or intergalactic jailbreaks. There were no mech battles or zombie warriors or mythical beasts or mystical archvillains or demon slayers or creature hunters or anything that was even remotely cool.

The only thing the *Silly Willy* comic strip offered was something much, much worse... *weekly life lessons*.

As Fatima screamed, "NOOOOOO!" the letters *N-O-O-O-O-O-!* appeared above her in a speech bubble.

CHAPTER 24
Mya & Madison

It was long past lunchtime, and the students of Classroom 13 were getting hungry. "I'm starving!" Teo moaned.

"We're more starving," Mya said.

"Yeah, we're twins, which means we're *twice* as hungry," Madison agreed.

Mya & Madison were twins. The two identical sisters had the same exact hair, the same exact clothes, and often the same exact thoughts. So when it was their turn with the ~~genie~~ djinn, they said the same exact wish at the same exact time.

"We wish for a lifetime supply of pizza—with extra cheese and anchovies!" Madison & Mya said.

"*Two* girls using only *one* wish?" The Grand Djinn shrugged. "Sure makes my job easier! Wish granted!"

When Mya & Madison got home, they found stacks of pizza boxes all over their front lawn. They grabbed the first box, opened it, and breathed in the delicious smell of fresh pizza.

They ate slice after slice of anchovy-and-extra-cheese pizza until it was time for bed. They woke up and had some more for a midnight snack. They even ate it cold for breakfast the next morning (which is—let's be honest—the best way to eat pizza).

After a few days, Mya & Madison discovered they were tired of eating pizza. "I...I don't think I want another slice," Madison said.

"Me either," Mya said.

"Oh no! You are going to keep eating until all this pizza is gone!" their parents said. "You wished it; you eat it!"

But there were pizza boxes everywhere. The kitchen had boxes to the ceiling. The living room had so many pizza pies you couldn't find the couch. Both Madison & Mya's matching bedrooms were full. Luckily, the house was air-conditioned.

But the pizzas outside—under the hot sun all day long—began to stink. The stench attracted seagulls from miles away (along with one mallard that looked like their friend Mark).

The neighbors complained about the smell—not to mention the bird poop on their cars from all the nasty seagulls.

Mya & Madison tried their best to eat more pizza, but it was more than they could stomach. They ate slice after slice until they made themselves sick.

"Let's give it away," their parents suggested. "We'll have a neighborhood pizza party and give it away for free."

"It will give me gas," one neighbor said.

"This is just unsanitary," a second neighbor added.

"Why'd you have to wish for anchovies? Who does that?!" the family next door asked. No one wanted the stinky old fish pizza.

Soon, the pizza began to mold and rot. More seagulls came, and cockroaches, too. Some people even said they'd seen a certain "Pizza Rat" arrive in town on a flight from New York City.

The neighbors formed an angry mob, but instead of pitchforks, they came waving regular forks around. (I guess it was supposed to be symbolic.) They demanded Madison & Mya find a way to destroy the remaining pizza slices. They didn't know what was worse—how much the town hated them, or how terrible the rotten pizzas smelled.

Mya & Madison hid from the world behind a wall of pizza boxes. They drank pink stomach medicine and wished they'd been smart enough to each keep a second wish instead of doubling down on just one. If they still had it, they would make the same exact wish—they'd wish to *never* eat or see or smell pizza ever again.

CHAPTER 25
Preeya

Preeya didn't like the idea of just *one* wish. She didn't like one of anything—she always wanted more.

Her family and friends knew that Preeya could be a little greedy sometimes. On her birthday, she couldn't just have one kind of birthday cake, she needed chocolate cake *and* vanilla cake *and* strawberry cake *and* ice-cream cake *and* a cookie cake *and* cupcakes.

Preeya's favorite word was "and." She always wanted more.

So now that she was face-to-face with the Grand Djinn, she didn't want to wish for one *measly* thing....

She wanted ALL THE THINGS!

So Preeya thought of something clever. Preeya smiled a wicked smile at the blue wish-maker and said, "I wish to have a huge birthday party *and* I want all the best presents *and* a new swimming pool *and* my own hotel to have a sleepover *and* all the clothes from my favorite store *and*..."

As Preeya kept going, the Grand Djinn saw through her trickery. She wasn't the first to try this stunt, and she wouldn't be the last. He shrugged. He wanted to see if she ran out of words or ran out of breath first.

"...*and* I want my favorite boy band to perform a private show for me *and* I want them to dedicate a song just to me *and* I want a diamond tiara *and* I want a bunch of dolphins *and* my own limo *and* the prettiest dress in the whole wide world *and* I want to be a princess *and...*"

Preeya started to get light-headed. She couldn't stop to breathe. She needed to keep going. "...*and* a real castle *and* a real royal wedding to a prince *and* another prince who wants to marry me even though I don't want to marry him *and* a horse-drawn carriage *and* two glass slippers *and* a new car for my sixteenth birthday *and* a chocolate-dipping fountain *and* more friends *and...*"

When Preeya stopped to take a breath, the djinn held his hand up to silence her. "*And* your wish is granted!"

Preeya was ecstatic. She couldn't wait for her one wish *for so many things* to come true. She turned around and stuck out her tongue at all the other students. She had fooled the djinn, who had fooled all the other students. Or so Preeya thought....

The djinn was the one smiling wickedly now. There was a *poof* of smoke. When it cleared, Preeya's face was pressed up against glass.

She looked outside and saw the rest of Classroom 13 and her fellow students staring down at her. The djinn had shrunk her and placed her inside a snow globe—along with everything else she had wished for.

It was a pity she asked for so much. With so many things, it was a painfully tight squeeze in there. Preeya could barely breathe.

"Mshhhhh...Lllinduhhhhh..." she tried to say, barely able to move her lips. "A lllittle helllllp, ppllleease...?"

Ms. Linda picked up Preeya's snow globe and placed it on her desk. It made a very nice paperweight.

CHAPTER 26
Ximena

Ximena had (what some people refer to as) the *travel bug*. This is just a weird way of saying Ximena liked to travel. There were no bugs involved.

Her family was poor, so they rarely went anywhere farther than the grocery store. In fact, Ximena had never left the town she was born in. She'd never even seen a different state.

With a global vacation in mind, Ximena told the ~~genie~~ djinn her desire: "I wish to take a trip around the world with my family."

The Grand Djinn snapped his blue fingers. Ximena and her entire family were magically transported onto a plane. They were thirty-nine thousand feet in the air, circling the globe.

"This is so exciting!" Ximena said, looking out the window at the clouds and ocean below. "Where are we going to land first?"

"We aren't," the flight attendant told her.

"What?!"

"This is Djinn Airlines. We're flying *around* the whole world—as you wished. We don't have a destination."

"But what about fuel?" Ximena asked, trying to think of any reason to get off the plane. "Eventually, we'll run out. We'll have to land to refuel, right?"

"Nope," the flight attendant said. "We have infinite fuel, infinite in-flight meals, infinite in-flight movies, and a nearly infinite wait to use the bathroom. Just like a real airline."

Ximena's family's smiles turned into frowns. They buckled in for the longest flight of their lives. They dined on peanuts, pretzels, and the same egg salad sandwiches for breakfast, lunch, and dinner every day for days. The air in the cabin always had the odor of a recycled fart. And true to the flight attendant's word, they never landed.

The plane just kept circling the globe. Ximena thought she saw a few famous sites but she couldn't be sure—everything looked ant-sized from this high up in the sky.

When she got bored, she watched an in-flight movie. Ironically, *Aladdin* was playing on every channel. When she got tired, Ximena slept (uncomfortably) sitting up. She realized she should have requested to fly first class. Coach was horrible.

When she had to go, *you know*, she waited

her turn, doing the *I need to pee* dance until her bladder felt like it would explode. And the bathrooms? Let's just say sharing the bathroom with two hundred people on a very long flight gets very, very gross.

It was a trip Ximena would never forget.

CHAPTER 27
Jacob

Jacob loves TV. When he isn't at school, he's binge-watching his favorite shows. If he's not viewing them on an actual television, he's watching them on his tablet or his phone or his computer. He even has a waterproof TV setup in the bathtub so he can stream shows in the shower.

(By the way, I do *not* recommend having a

tablet anywhere near your bathtub. Never mind the possibility of electrocution, tablets are very expensive. And stores will *not* accept "innocent bath-time accident" as a reason for return, no matter how much I—I mean, *you*—whine or cry or pitch a tantrum. Trust me.)

Anyhoo. When Jacob's turn to make a wish came, he said, "I wish to be a TV star!"

Instead of just quickly granting the wish, the Grand Djinn paused to think. (Apparently, the blue man knew all about making Hollywood dreams come true.)

"What kind of star?" the djinn asked. "The party-all-the-time kind? The fat-sad-former-child-star kind? Or the mega-famous-superstar kind?"

"Mega-famous-superstar, please," Jacob said.

So the djinn made Jacob famous. Mega-super famous.

How famous *is* mega-super famous?

Well, as soon as the magic dust cleared, an army of paparazzi appeared. Paparazzi—also known as terrible and devious photographers who will do anything to snap a photo—started snapping his photo. The camera flashes were blinding.

Jacob ran out of Classroom 13, out of the school, and toward home. The paparazzi chased him. When he fell, they snapped pictures of him and said, "Celebrity klutz! Great headline!" Jacob was lucky his ankle wasn't broken.

He finally managed to hide behind Mrs. Crabapple's house. Her laundry was hanging up in her backyard, and he hid behind a giant dress. Looking up, he realized he was surrounded by ladies underwear. "Ack!" he gasped, and made a run for it.

But when he got home, there was no way to get in. His house was mobbed by legions of adoring fans. Every time a car passed by, his fans screamed in excitement, thinking it was him. These fans called themselves "Ja-Cubs for Jacob." The Ja-Cubs had handmade signs and shirts that read JACOB IS MY HERO, or JA-CUB 4 LYFE, or JACOB, WILL YOU MARRY ME?!

Jacob was hiding across the street, trying to figure out how to get into his house unnoticed.

Hours and hours passed. Finally, the Ja-Cubs set up tents and sleeping bags and went to sleep. Very carefully, he tiptoed between the snoring fans and snuck into his own house.

Is this what stars live through every day? Jacob wondered. *It's exhausting.* At least it felt good to be home, away from the craziness of new famousness.

That's when his parents turned on the light and surprised him by giving him a hug. (You see, Jacob's parents were usually rather private and antisocial parents. They mumbled maybe one or two words to him each month. It was usually "no.")

"Hi, honey. Why are you home so early?" his mom asked.

"Early? It's after midnight!" Jacob said, surprised he wasn't grounded.

"Son, you're a mega-famous superstar. You should be at work right now," his dad said.

"Work?!"

"Of course. All mega-famous superstars work twenty-three hours a day. That's how they stay famous."

"I don't want to work that much!" Jacob cried. "When will I watch TV?!"

"TV? Oh, sweetie." His parents giggled. "Mega-famous superstars don't watch TV. They don't have time. They're too busy being *on* TV."

Jacob fell to his knees dramatically and screamed, "NOOOOOOOOOOOOOO!"

CHAPTER 28
Ethan

To no one's surprise, Ethan didn't know what to wish for yet. This was because Ethan was always "of two minds" about everything. As soon as he started to make a choice (for example, picking Swiss cheese over cheddar cheese), he'd convince himself to change his mind. (Cheddar was clearly better; it was sharper!) Then he'd change it again. (No, it's too sharp! Swiss is subtle. Swiss all the way!)

This may seem nutty to you and me, but it was totally normal for Ethan. It was just how his brain worked—he liked debating things.

Ethan was happy to be at the back of the wish line. He needed extra time to weigh his wishing options.

So—while you've been reading this whole time, and his classmates have been making their wishes—Ethan has been arguing with himself at the back of the line trying to decide what to wish for.

I love sports. Perhaps I should wish to own all the football teams in the world. Then I could watch the games anytime I'd want and I'd be stinking rich. Then again, I prefer baseball....Then again, it would be cool to own Super Bowl Sundays. Then again, baseball is America's favorite pastime....

And so on and on it went in Ethan's head.

When it came time for Ethan to make his wish, he still hadn't made up his mind. The Grand Djinn grew more impatient by the second.

"Hurry up. I need a nap. It's been a long day of wish granting."

"I'm sorry, I'm sorry! Just, uh, I think, um..." Ethan stuttered. Finally, he blurted out, "*Ugh, I wish I could think of something!*"

"Wish granted!" the Grand Djinn said.

Just then, an idea popped into Ethan's head—the perfect wish.

Though what that wish is, we will never know.

"Okay, I know what to wish for!" Ethan exclaimed.

"Nuh-uh, man," the Grand Djinn said, shaking his head. "You just used your wish to wish for an idea. Next!"

Ethan drove his wheelchair to the wall so he could bang his head on it. He was furious with himself for having been so careless.

No, he wasn't mad. He was sad.

No, mad, he thought. *I'm mad. Well...maybe*

more sad. But why was the djinn so literal? That makes me mad! I used up my wish on a technicality. No more wish. That makes me sad. No...it makes me mad!

The great sad-versus-mad debate would continue for several days—until Ethan had a new idea about how to get his wish back....

CHAPTER 29
Olivia

"I wish for world peace," Olivia said.

"What?!" The djinn was shocked by Olivia's wish. "That wish isn't selfish at all. No one ever wishes for that. It's so...so...*selfless*!"

"Not really," Olivia said. "I am the smartest student in school. I know better than to waste my wish on something silly. I needed to make a wish that I can put on my future college applications that will help me get accepted at the best schools."

"Well played," the djinn said. He snapped his fingers, and—miraculously—all war and violence and anger vanished from the earth.

CHAPTER 30
Second-Chance Santiago

Days went by, and the students of Classroom 13 were—for the most part—very miserable. They'd had a chance at making a wish (*any wish!*), and somehow they each had screwed it up.

Well, except for Mason. He loved his flashlight. And Earl, who loved his sunflower seeds.

Oh, and of course, Olivia. She wished for

world peace. And the whole world was at peace.

After several days, Ethan had finally thought of a plan to get his wish back....Ethan snuck out his cell phone and texted Santiago:

DUDE. R u still sick?

a djinn is here granting wishes. he was gonna leave but Ms. L insisted you get your wish first.

Get here ASAP.

B rite there!

A few minutes later, Santiago Santos appeared in the doorway of Classroom 13. He was over the flu, but now he had strep throat. With a runny nose and puffy face, and still wearing his bathrobe, Santiago dragged himself to the front of the class and picked up the djinn's lamp. He gave it a rub.

"Who's this?" the Grand Djinn asked.

"I'm Santia—*cough*!" After a phlegmy coughing fit, he continued. "I rode my bike all the way here so I could make my wish."

"Sorry, pal," the Grand Djinn said. "I'm finished granting wishes to this classroom full of weirdos."

"Weird? Who's weird?" Liam asked through his fishbowl.

"What a rude djinn!" Ms. Linda said. "That's the last time I bring a strange lamp into class."

"Come on!" Santiago begged. "One last wish, please?!"

"You weren't here when Ms. Linda rubbed my lamp," the djinn said. "So no wish for you."

"No wish?! *Ugh*. I wish I'd been here that

day!" Santiago said, accidentally rubbing the other lamp on Ms. Linda's desk with his butt.

In a burst of golden light, Ava the Djinn appeared. "Hey, Santi! Still sick, huh? Shoulda wished to be healthy, but I'll grant your wish."

"What wish?" Santiago asked.

"You just wished you'd been here that day. And your wish is my command!"

Ava snapped her fingers. Suddenly, time began to go *backward*!

All of Classroom 13's wishes were undone: Ximena's family found themselves off the plane and back home. Emma's parents were divorced (and happy) again. Ava was no longer a ~~genie~~ djinn, and Mark shed his feathers.

Unfortunately, even Olivia's wish was undone. No more world peace. See ya later, world peace! (Hopefully...but probably not.)

It was as if the last few days had never happened at all—except that everyone remembered.

Everyone and everything was back to the way it had been—except Santiago was in class that morning, despite being sick. Santiago sniffled.

Even Ms. Linda's swollen lip was back. She winced from the bee sting. "Aww gweat, my wip is swowwen again!"

This was Ethan's chance to redo his wish—his plan had worked. He shouted to the class, "Okay, this time, let's all think hard on our wishes before Ms. Linda rubs the lamp for the first time. We can all have new wishes!"

The whole class cheered. It was almost too perfect.

As Ms. Linda picked up the lamp, Santiago let out a horrific and loud snot-filled sneeze that startled everyone. *"ACCCHHHOOOOOOO!"* It scared Ms. Linda so bad, she dropped the djinn's lamp, and it shattered on the floor into a million pieces.

The djinn shouted, "I'm free!" and flew away.

The rest of the do-over day was just like any other day.

For the kids, it was a long stretch of *wishing* for the bell to ring.

For Ms. Linda, it was a long wait of *wishing* for some topical cream to numb her throbbing lip.

And for the 13th Classroom, it was a long eternity of *wishing* someone, anyone, could hear it. But the Classroom only spoke at a whisper. That's why no one heard it begging for a chance to ask the djinn for a wish.

It would've wished for the one thing it wanted most in the world—but that's a tale for another time.

CHAPTER 31
Your Chapter

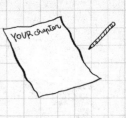

That's right—it's your turn!

Grab some paper and a writing utensil. (Not a fork, silly. Try a pencil or pen.) Or if you have one of those fancy computer doo-hickeys, use that. Now tell me...

If YOU had one magic wish, what would YOU wish for?!

When you're done, share it with your teacher, your family, and your friends. (Don't forget your pets! Pets like to hear stories, too.) You can even ask your parents to send me your chapter at the address below.

HONEST LEE

LITTLE, BROWN BOOKS FOR YOUNG READERS

1290 Avenue of the Americas

New York, NY 10104

★ BOOK 3 ★
in the Classroom 13 Series

THE FANTASTIC and Terrible FAME OF CLASSROOM 13

By **Honest Lee** & **Matthew J. Gilbert**
Art by **Joelle Dreidemy**

LITTLE, BROWN AND COMPANY
New York • Boston

CONTENTS

PSSST! HEY, YOU! FOR MY CHAPTER, YOU MIGHT WANT TO REWRITE MY CODE—BACKWARDS.

CHAPTER 1
Unfamous Ms. Linda

When *not*-famous schoolteacher Ms. Linda LaCrosse woke up Monday morning, she decided it would be another boring day. Little did she know how wrong she was.

First, she had been up late grading papers and forgotten to set her alarm. Ms. Linda didn't realize it until her cat bit her nose and woke her up. "I'm going to be late! Again!"

Second, she put her right shoe on her left foot, and her left shoe on her right foot. Then she brushed her hair, put on her clothes, and hopped in the shower. As she rushed to school, she wondered why she was soaking wet.

You might think Ms. Linda was quite silly and *should* be famous, but she was *not*. (Not anymore...) Ms. Linda is not a pop star or a TV actress or a soccer player or a famous writer. (Like me, Honest Lee. What's that? Yes, I *am* too famous!)

But Ms. Linda *is* related to someone who knows lots of famous people—her cousin Lucy LaRoux, who is a very famous agent who works at the Ace Agent Agency in Hollywood.

What's an agent? Well, agents are the people who represent pop stars and TV actresses and soccer players and famous writers. They help them get work and help them stay famous. They also charge a great deal of money for their services. (Make a mental note, as this will be important later.)

"Ms. Linda! You are late again!" said the principal. His arms were crossed, and he was tapping his shoe against the floor tiles.

"I know, I know!" Ms. Linda said. She ran past him and straight to her class. As you might know, the students of the 13th Classroom can be quite a handful. And so Ms. Linda expected them to be causing trouble. Instead, she found them all sitting quietly, listening to a story told by someone sitting on her desk.

"...and so I said, 'Don't you dare!' And do you know what Ten Bears did? He ate the entire tarantula."

The whole class laughed.

"Though bears prefer honey, I suppose one would eat a spider," Ms. Linda said. "How is that funny?"

"No, Ms. Linda," said Teo. "*Ten Bears* isn't an

actual bear. He's a human boy and he's *famous*! I want to be just like him."

"What's he famous for?" Ms. Linda asked.

"For being on the Internet," Teo said.

"But *what* is he famous for?" Ms. Linda asked. "What does he *do*?"

"He makes videos. On the Internet," Teo said.

"I don't understand this generation," Ms. Linda said.

"And that's why you're *not* a famous agent like me," said Lucy LaRoux, famous agent of Ace Agent Agency.

"Lucy?! What are you doing here?" Ms. Linda said, surprised to see her cousin outside of Hollywood.

"Well, my boss said we needed more kid stars, and I thought to myself, *Where do I find a bunch of brats—ur, I mean, children?* Naturally I thought of you. You work with children, so here I am. I plan to make all these kids famous!"

The students in Ms. Linda's class screamed with glee. (Except for Yuna. She had no interest in being famous.)

Of Ms. Linda's twenty-seven students, twenty-six of them were present. Not so surprisingly, Santiago was out again. (He wasn't exactly "sick," but his mom insisted he go to the hospital—just because one of his fingers *fell off* his hand. He didn't think it was that big of a deal, but his mother quite disagreed.)

Of the twenty-six students who were in class, twenty-five of them were paying attention to the famous agent who worked at Ace Agent Agency. They never paid this much attention to Ms. Linda. She crossed her arms.

"Lucy, this is a classroom," Ms. Linda said. "You can't just walk in here and distract my students. They are here to learn. Not become famous."

"Can't we do both?" Ava asked.

"I don't know...." Ms. Linda answered.

"You don't want to hold them back, do you?" Lucy asked. "Just because *your* fifteen minutes of fame didn't work out—"

"Ms. Linda was famous?!" Jayden Jason asked, shocked.

"For what?!" asked Chloe.

"She hasn't told you?" Lucy asked. "Well, let me fill you in...."

CHAPTER 2

Infamous Ms. Linda

Once upon a time, little Linda LaCrosse was the same age as her students. And more than anything, she loved to sing. She sang when she did her chores. She sang when she brushed her teeth. She even sang when she slept.

One day, her family went for a visit to Hollywood, and an agent heard her singing. "What a beautiful singing voice you have!" he said. "I am certain I can make you an opera star!"

And he did.

Little Linda LaCrosse became quite famous. She sang at very important opera houses all around the world. She even got a singing coach. This coach pushed her to sing harder and deeper and higher. It turned out little Linda LaCrosse could sing so high that it made glass break.

Well, at the peak of her fame, she was sent to Beijing, China, to sing at the National Grand Theater—which was made entirely of glass. Her coach kept telling her, "You have to sing harder and deeper and higher than ever before!"

And so she did.

And the entire opera house shattered.

"And *that* was the end of Ms. Linda's singing career," Lucy explained, finishing her story.

"That's wonderful!" said Liam.

"That's horrible," said Ximena.

"I think it's neat," said Lily.

"The famous painter Andy Warhol once said,

'In the future, everyone will be world-famous for fifteen minutes.' And that was *my* fifteen minutes of fame," said Ms. Linda. "Sometimes being famous can quickly lead to being *infamous*."

"Isn't that the same thing?" William asked.

"Not at all," Ms. Linda said. " 'Famous' means being known for something good. 'Infamous' means being known for something *bad*."

"It's better to be infamous than not famous at all," said Preeya.

"Oh, I quite disagree," Ms. Linda said. "I'm still not allowed back into China after what I did."

"Enough talking about you," Lucy LaRoux said. "It's time to make these children celebrities."

"I don't think that's a good idea," Ms. Linda said to her cousin.

"On the contrary." Lucy smiled. "You just said in the future, everyone would be famous for fifteen minutes. Well, the future is now. Who wants to be famous?"

The entire class—except Yuna—cheered and shouted with excitement.

"Fantastic! All of you step right up and sign this contract that makes ~~you my servants~~ me your agent, and we'll get started on making each of you famous."

"What's the contract say?" Ms. Linda asked her cousin. She tried to read the fine print, but it was itsy-bitsy-teeny-tiny....

"Don't worry about it!" Lucy snapped.

Ms. Linda begged the students not to sign the contracts. But as students often do with their teachers, no one listened.

CHAPTER 3
Jayden Jason

Jayden was excited about being famous. He didn't know what he'd be famous for, but he figured Lucy would know. And she did.

"You must be Jayden Jason James, aka Triple J," Lucy said with a sly smile. "I hear you're the most popular kid in school and have a huge following online. I see you also have an undeniable star quality about you. Let's do lunch."

"Doing lunch" in Hollywood means making

deals at a fancy outdoor café with caviar and paparazzi. Here in school, it means making deals at the cafeteria with day-old fish sticks and that one weird kid from Classroom 10 watching them eat.

"Now, I want the *Triple* in Triple J to mean something. Do you know what a 'triple threat' is?" Lucy asked. Jayden shook his head and ate a fish stick.

"It means you're famous for three things instead of one. You can sing *and* act *and* model. Maybe you could act in a movie about a model who sings! Maybe you could even write the movie, do the soundtrack, and design the clothes. What do you think about fragrance? If you can do seven things, you could be a *septuple* threat!"

"Sure, I can do whatever," Jayden said.

Dollar signs lit up in Lucy's eyes.

And somehow Jayden did do it all—*and* he made it look easy.

Triple J wrote his first screenplay that night. The next morning, he filmed all his movie scenes. That afternoon, he recorded his first album, then began to design clothes for his new fashion label. After that, he took a private jet to Italy to model in his first fashion show the next morning. He was a natural.

Within a week, he was bigger than a star—he was a global phenomenon.

His brand name—Triple J—was in magazines, in TV commercials, on the Internet, in movies, everywhere. In almost no time at all, he became a *tredecuple* threat. Meaning, he had *thirteen* different talents. It's almost as if he had *clones* helping him out.

If you've ever seen his movie, the credits say:

A TRIPLE J PRODUCTION STARRING **TRIPLE J**
IN A FILM BY **TRIPLE J** ORIGINAL SOUNDTRACK BY **TRIPLE J**
AND ORIGINAL DANCE CHOREOGRAPHY BY **TRIPLE J**
EDITED BY **SOME WEIRDO**
PRODUCED, DIRECTED, AND CATERED BY **TRIPLE J**

Yes, Triple J could do anything. He'd even gone into the catering business. In between filming scenes, he grilled omelets for the local homeless shelter. "Triple cheese omelets coming right up!" he'd say.

He quickly became Lucy's biggest money-maker. The new deals were pouring in and were going to make ~~Jayden~~ Lucy rich! All Triple J had to do was sign a new contract.

"No thanks," Triple J said.

Lucy nearly choked on her triple grilled cheese. "What?!"

"I'm tired of the biz. Feeding the homeless has shown me there are more important things in life than starring in movies and recording hit records and sleeping on big piles of money. Giving is truly better than getting."

Lucy was furious. "You have lost it! You can't just leave! You can't quit! I have you under contract!"

"So sue me." He laughed. Lucy tried, but Triple J had given all his money to charity, hopped on a plane to Tibet, and become a monk.

There, he learned to meditate. But after a few weeks of absolute quiet, he became absolutely bored. So he came home.

CHAPTER 4
Preeya

"Who's next?" famous agent Lucy LaRoux asked.

Preeya stood on her desk and addressed the room: "I am! I'm the prettiest girl in class..." (This was not true.)

"...and one of the smartest," she continued. (Nor was this.)

"...and I normally tell you guys everything

about my life..." (This *was* true, though most of the students found it quite irritating.)

"...but I've been keeping a major secret from all of you for quite some time," Preeya said. "I'm ready to come clean. I can actually SING! Yes! Me! Just when you thought I couldn't be any more talented or gorgeous or wonderful, here I am, rocking you through song!"

Preeya began to sing. Many of the students covered their ears, expecting to hear a voice like nails on the chalkboard. Instead, everyone was impressed. Preeya was good. Not amazing, mind you, but decent. Lucy saw potential— meaning, she didn't think Preeya was a natural talent, but she could certainly be *molded* into something.

"I'm ready to be a star!" Preeya announced.

First, Lucy phoned the Ace Agent Agency and had them set up some tour dates. Second, she had Preeya record an album and leak it online.

And third, Lucy booked an appointment with famous fashionista Farrah Far-Out-There.

"Why'd you call Farrah? I already have a look!" Preeya said.

"Oh, dollface," Lucy said, "in today's media industry, it's not enough to be a good singer. You have to have a *gimmick* if you want to keep trending."

"What's going to be my gimmick?" Preeya asked.

"Fashion, fashion, fashion!" Lucy said.

For Preeya's first round of public appearances, Farrah Far-Out-There made a dress entirely of raw poultry and fish. Chicken cutlets made her blouse while shiny fish made up her skirt. She wore anchovy earrings and bracelets made of chicken sausage. Preeya felt disgusting, but she smiled for the cameras.

Sophia and Chloe showed up—to boycott her animal-carcass fashion. The next day, Preeya and her chicken-fish dress sizzled all over social media.

Farrah Far-Out-There's next crazy outfit for Preeya was simple: It was a beehive dress—made of an actual beehive with actual bees living inside it. The bees stung Preeya over and over. But once again, she smiled for the cameras.

Sophia and Chloe showed up again—this time to boycott her abuse of bees. This only helped the buzz. Preeya's song "Queen Bee" made number one on the charts.

Next, Farrah Far-Out-There designed a dress made out of jellyfish and porcupines. "Noooooooope!" Preeya said. "No way. I don't mind some pain, but that's going too far."

Instead, Farrah Far-Out-There crafted a suit made of 100 percent authentic New York City garbage. She stitched together rotten banana peels, used Chinese-food cartons, and pieces of gum scraped off the sidewalks.

Sure enough, the paparazzi fought in a photo frenzy over Preeya's hot *trash du jour* look. She stunk up the red carpet with it, posing for pic after pic. She may have smelled like a landfill, but the only thing that filled her nostrils was the sweet smell of success.

Finally, it was time for Preeya to take the stage. The lights came up, the crowd roared, and that's when she looked out at all those faces....

Preeya suddenly couldn't move.

All those people. Staring. At her.

There had to be forty thousand eyeballs looking straight at her. Some of them weren't even blinking. Preeya felt like she was about to faint. This wasn't like singing in the shower or performing for her classmates at school—this was different. This was TOO. MANY. PEOPLE.

Preeya instantly remembered why she kept her singing talents hidden—because she had terrible *stage fright*.

She dropped the microphone, ran off stage, and never came back out.

CHAPTER 5
Dev

Dev ran up to Lucy and waved his fingers in front of her face. "Check it out," he said. "Pretty amazing, huh?"

"What am I looking at?" Lucy asked.

"My fast fingers," Dev said. "I'm the best video game player on this side of the planet. Can you make me famous now?"

"What else can you do?" Lucy asked.

"Um...I can play piano."

Dev took a seat at the classroom piano and began playing. He was so good, it brought tears to Ms. Linda's eyes. It turned out that years and years of playing video games had made Dev's fingers incredibly strong, fast, and agile. (He also happened to be a musical prodigy.)

"Now we're cooking." Lucy smiled. "I'm thinking Carnegie Hall."

Dev auditioned, and the classical music judges wept. They agreed to let him play every night of the week—for the rest of his life.

To keep his fingers as nimble as possible, the Ace Agent Agency hired a piano coach. He was an old Russian man named Vladimir Vliolin, and he had a reputation for being strict.

How strict? Well, for starters, Vladimir told Dev he was no longer allowed to play video games.

"WHAT?!" Dev asked, freaking out. "But games are my life!"

"No. Music is life now! Your precious fingers

must rest when they not play piano," Vladimir insisted. "Video games in zee trash!"

So Dev did the sensible thing....

"I quit," he told Lucy.

"But you haven't even played one show yet," she growled. "Your music career hasn't even started! You're not even technically famous. And most important, I haven't gotten any money yet!"

Dev didn't care. Not when the hottest new game of the year was waiting for him at home. Tonight would be an all-night gaming marathon of *Teddy Bear Bashers: Space Capades 2: Comet Cubs.* He cracked his fingers and stretched. Being famous just wasn't as fun as playing video games.

CHAPTER 6
Yuna

Yuna did *not* want to be famous. Ms. Linda told her cousin this, but Lucy LaRoux didn't believe it. She said, "Everyone wants to be famous for something!"

Yuna wrote on a piece of paper and held it up. It said: I DON'T.

"Come on, kid," Lucy LaRoux said. "Don't play games with me. What do you want to be famous for? Tell me!"

Yuna scribbled something on a piece of paper and handed it to Lucy. This is what her note said:

.EM OT NOITNETTA DETNAWNU

GNIWARD ERA UOY .ESAELP YAWA

OG WON .SKNAHT ON .HAEY OS

.TUO SI YTIRBELEC A GNIEB

SNAEM TAHT .EM EZINGOCER

NAC ENO ON ,YAD ENO YPS DOOG

A EB OT GNIOG MA I FI DNA

,YPS A EB OT TNAW I .YLLAUTCA

ETISOPPO EHT ETIUQ TNAW I

.SUOMAF EB OT TNAW TON OD I

Lucy threw her hands up. "Fine! Then I give up!" As she wandered away to find a student who *did* want to be famous, Yuna sat back and smiled.

CHAPTER 7
Benji

Benji got dressed up for his meeting with Lucy. Instead of just wearing the clothes he came to school in, he slipped out to his locker for an outfit change. When it was his turn, Lucy found him sporting head-to-toe "football" gear.

Benji spit out his mouth guard and said, "I love two things: unicorns and football. But since there's already a world-famous unicorn, I want to be a famous football player!"

"But you're not wearing a football uniform." Lucy snorted. "You're wearing a *soccer* uniform."

Benji rolled his eyes. "Americans call it soccer, but the rest of the world calls it football. FIFA stands for *Fédération Internationale de Football Association*. One day, I dream of playing in the FIFA World Cup."

Lucy checked the calendar on her phone. "We better hurry, then. The World Cup is this weekend."

That weekend, famous agent Lucy LaRoux escorted Benji to Brazil for the final games of the tournament. Tens of thousands of ~~soccer~~ football fans sat in sold-out arenas, anxiously awaiting the first kick.

Lucy used her Ace Agent Agency connections to get Benji on the roster and in the game. He was now playing for Brazil. When Benji ran out onto the field, his heart swelled with pride. Sure, Benji didn't have muscle, skill, or years of ~~soccer~~ football experience—but he didn't let that bother him. He was about to play professional ball with his heroes.

As the Germans (the opposing team) took the field, they looked at Benji. Some laughed, others growled, and one said, "You're dead meat."

Benji gulped.

His teammates gave him a look of concern. The central midfielder said, "Good luck, kid."

As the referee blew the whistle, the game began. After almost two whole minutes playing the game, the striker kicked the ball to Benji. This was the happiest moment of Benji's young life.

And that was the last thing Benji remembered before everything went black.

Benji woke up in a hospital in a head-to-toe full-body cast. Little Benji got *destroyed* out there.

That's what happens when an untrained kid gets stomped by hundreds of pounds of professional German ~~soccer players~~ footballers.

He broke nearly every single bone in his body. So why was he smiling? His team had won. And since he was technically on the team—even if only for one hundred and twenty seconds—they let him have the trophy. It shined brighter than anything he'd ever seen.

CHAPTER 8
Mason

"I want to be a famous actress!" Mason said. Mason was very good at sports. But he wasn't so bright.

"You mean an *actor*," Lucy said.

"No way. Actresses get all the best roles and win big awards. That's what I want," Mason said.

"But you're a *boy*," Lucy explained to Mason.

"So?!" Mason said, offended. "Boys can be actresses, too!"

Lucy shrugged. "Fine. Let's get your headshot."

Mason ducked under his desk. "What?! Don't shoot me!"

"No, a 'headshot' is just a picture of your face. All actors—and actresses—have them. I send them out to different studio people. Whoever likes your headshot invites you to try out for a role."

"I like bread rolls," Mason said, "with lots of butter."

"Right," Lucy said.

Mason wasn't the smartest (or sharpest) tool in the shed, but he was photogenic. As soon as Lucy sent out his headshot, he got invited to try out for over a dozen TV shows.

Unfortunately, Mason couldn't act his way out of a box. And I mean that very seriously. On his first audition, he got stuck inside a box for thirty minutes and couldn't find his way out.

"Just take the box off your head!" Lucy snapped. She was very frustrated.

At Mason's next audition, he got stuck in

another box. At the third TV set, he followed a cat into a box, and they both got stuck. Some of the film crew started shooting videos of Mason. They couldn't stop laughing.

"This is hilarious!" one of the camera people said. "This should be on the Internet."

This gave Lucy a great idea. She put Mason on the Internet. He was going to be huge. They'd give him his own channel. Maybe they could call it Box Boy.

At the end of the week, Lucy called Mason. "I'm afraid I can't represent you. You're just not fame material. You only got fourteen views on social media. That's less than my goldfish."

"Fourteen views," Mason said. "*Fourteen* views on the *Interwebs?!*" He started jumping up and down and screaming. "*I'm famous! I'm famous. Four. Teen. Views! Mom, I'm a famous actress!!*"

"Of course you are, dear," his mom said.

Lucy hung up the phone.

CHAPTER 9
Isabella

Isabella was very strong. Not normal strong, like kids who like to play outside or exercise. I mean action-hero strong. I suppose that's what happens when you spend all your free time at the stables, wrangling wild horses and riding bulls.

"I want to be a pro wrestler," Isabella told Lucy.

"I like it! Girl power!" Lucy said. "Have you thought of what your wrestler name will be?"

"They'll call me DIZZABELLA—because I'll hit you so hard, I'll make you DIZZY!"

"All right! Time to wrestle some money into *my* bank account!" Lucy said before quickly correcting herself. "I mean, *your* bank account! We're doing this for you. Um, let's go!"

To protect her identity (and hide the fact that she was a minor), Isabella wore a *luchador* mask—a colorful disguise made famous by wrestlers in Mexico and other Spanish-speaking countries.

The Ace Agent Agency arranged Dizzabella's first match against Body Slam Sam. When Dizzabella entered the ring, people laughed at her small size. Body Slam Sam was more than five times bigger than her.

But once the bell rang, it didn't matter. Dizzabella slapped Sam silly and then body-slammed him so hard, he farted a hole right through his wrestling shorts. The crowd was now chortling at him.

When the bell rang, Dizzabella could hardly believe she'd beaten the farts out of a three-hundred-pound muscleman.

"Wow, that was... *easy*," she told the TV cameras.

"You heard it here first, folks!" the ringside reporter told TV viewers. "Dizzabella says destroying Body Slam Sam was easy!"

After her surprise win, the Pro Wrestling Association invited Dizzabella to compete in the championship match against undefeated champ Dr. Dynamite, the circuit's baddest bad boy. The match took place in Las Vegas, in an arena of fifty thousand wrestling fans—and eleven people who just happened to be there for the all-you-can-eat pancake buffet.

When she heard the bell, Dizzabella charged.

She went with the Mongolian forehead chop. It barely grazed Dr. Dynamite, yet he crashed to the ground. "Please don't hurt me anymore, Dizzabella! Please!" he begged.

Dizzabella looked at her hands. Was she that strong? She paused for a moment, thinking of how odd it all was. *This weakling is the world champ*, she thought. *Earl the Hamster is tougher than this clown.*

Wrestler after wrestler, she defeated with ease. But with each win, she began to suspect something wasn't right—she just couldn't place her finger on it.

Before she knew it, the title bout was down to Dizzabella and her personal wrestling hero, Mountain Man Maniac McGee. There was no way she could take him down. He was a giant!

But Dizzabella had her eyes on the prize: the golden championship belt. If she wanted to wear it, she knew she had to keep fighting.

As soon as the bell rang, Dizzabella used the ropes like a slingshot to fling herself forward. She missed Maniac McGee on the first pass, but she climbed the ropes, did a corkscrew shooting star press, and knocked him so hard that he spun over the ropes and crashed facedown into the maple syrup bucket at the buffet line. He was knocked out cold.

The entire audience stood and cheered. Except for the eleven people who were just there for the pancakes. They were upset about the spilled syrup.

The announcer held Dizzabella's arm up in the air and proclaimed, "Your new heavyweight champion of the worrrrrrld: DIZZABELLA!!"

They gave her the giant gold belt. It was the happiest moment of her life. So why was something bothering her?

Lucy pulled her backstage. "You did great, kid! We have endorsements coming out the wazoo!"

"I can't believe it was so easy to beat Maniac McGee," Dizzabella said.

"I can," Lucy said. "It's all fake! There was no way you were going to lose!"

"WHAT?!"

"All that body-slamming and kicking? Fake. The tension between rivals? Fake. Heck, even this gold belt? Fake! The winners are all decided beforehand. Good thing they picked you to win, huh?"

Isabella couldn't believe the whole thing was staged. She felt like such a fraud. She wanted to win for real, not for fake.

So she body-slammed Lucy. For real.

CHAPTER 10
Santiago

You're probably wondering why Santiago's finger fell off. I'll tell you.

Most of the time, Santiago was sick, sneezing, snotting, and snoring all over the place. But for once, he woke up and felt great. The medicines his doctors prescribed hadn't worked, but his grandma's famous chicken soup sure had. His recent flu/cold/allergy thing was finally gone.

"I'm actually hungry today!" he told his mom. "Can I have a sandwich instead of soup today?"

"Of course," his mom said. "Give me just one minute, and I'll make it for you."

"I can make it!" Santiago said.

"Why don't you let me make it?" his mom asked. "Your father just had the knives sharpened the other day, and they're very sharp."

"I'll be careful," Santiago said.

Except that he wasn't careful. He was watching TV while he made his sandwich. So when he went to cut the crust off his sandwich, well...

...instead...

...he cut off...

(you know)

...HIS FINGER.

Ouch.

Don't worry. They sewed it back on. It's as good as new. Except for the uncontrollable twitching—which makes picking his nose very difficult.

CHAPTER 11
Sophia

Sophia is a tree hugger. That means she hugs trees. Literally.

But she also protects them. And not just trees, but animals and oceans and grass and pretty much anything on the planet that is natural.

So when Lucy asked her what she wanted to be famous for, Sophia smiled wide and said, "I want to save the planet."

"I like it," Lucy said. "Go with it!"

The Ace Agent Agency drove Sophia to a local construction site where they were tearing down a forest to put up a new business building. When Sophia saw this, she was furious. She shouted, "What did these woods ever do to you?!"

Sophia was so angry, she chained herself to the trees. "You can't knock down the rest of the forest without running me over. So take that!"

Within an hour, every news crew in the state had showed up to interview Sophia. "I just want to help clean up the world," Sophia explained. That night, she let all the air out of the tractor tires.

"I was expecting a peaceful protest," Lucy said, "but this works even better."

Next, the Ace Agent Agency flew Sophia to an oil field where they were drilling for oil. Once again, she chained herself up. This time, she yelled, "Quit stealing from the earth!" Once again, the news crews showed up to interview her. And that night, she gunked up all the drills with lots and lots of chewing gum.

After that, the Ace Agent Agency boated her to a fishing village, where she put on a scuba suit and chained herself to the fishing boats. "Leave the little fishies alone!" she shouted. News crews came again. With so many cameras watching her, Sophia felt something *snap!* Overcome with rage, she sank the fishing boats. And it was all caught on film.

The next morning, Lucy called her up and said, "Great news on the news! You're famous! They're calling you the Eco-Warrior."

Sophia read the headline:

ECO-WARRIOR TERRORIZES LOCAL FISHING TOWN. SINKS BOATS AND PUTS WORKERS OUT OF WORK.

"Oh no," Sophia said. "I didn't mean to make people lose their jobs!"

"But it's helping the planet!" Lucy said. "You want to help the planet, don't you?"

"I guess so," Sophia said, not so sure.

"Well, people all over the world are looking to you for the next step in saving the planet. I'm thinking Eco-Warrior T-shirts and Eco-Warrior posters and...how about an Eco-Warrior Million Person March?! You can march to the nation's capital and demand better treatment of plants."

"If it will help the earth..." Sophia said.

So the next week, Sophia arrived in Washington, D.C., by helicopter. There, she led a Million Person March to save the planet. But as the millions of people marched toward the Capitol, Sophia saw they were trampling the grass.

"Walk on the sidewalks!" Sophia shouted, but no one heard her. They were protesting too loudly.

By the time the millions of people had finished their march, they had killed the grass *and* left a trail of trash behind them.

"What have I done?!" Sophia yelled in anguish. For the next several weeks, Sophia cleaned up the trash, replanted every blade of grass that had been destroyed, and told Lucy she quit. She tore up her contract—and then recycled it.

CHAPTER 12
Ethan

Famous agent Lucy LaRoux was annoyed with these kids quitting on her. She didn't understand how wanting to lead a happy, normal life was more important than money. It was a ridiculous notion. She took a deep breath and went to the next student.

Now, if you know Ethan, you know he has a hard time making up his mind. When he found out he could be famous for something, he immediately thought of two different things but couldn't decide which.

"I either want to be a basketball player or a daredevil stuntman," Ethan explained to Lucy. "What do you think I would be better at?"

"Seriously?" Lucy asked. "Um, neither. You're in a wheelchair."

"EXCUSE ME?!" Ms. Linda and Sophia and Benji and Isabella and Mark roared at Lucy at the same time. They all crossed their arms and glared at her in outrage.

"Ethan can be anything he wants to be!" Ms. Linda said.

"And he can do anything he wants to!" Sophia added.

"You're a horrible person," added Benji.

"I agree. I *am* horrible!" Lucy smiled. "That's what makes me such a good agent. As for you, Ethan, let's go with daredevil stuntman. Show me what you've got."

With Ace Agent Agency's help, Ethan arranged a series of stunts, each bigger than the next.

First, he went down the highest roller coaster in the world—in his wheelchair. Next, he jumped over twenty cars and through twelve hoops of fire—in his wheelchair. After that, he walked a tightrope between two skyscrapers, eighty stories up—in his wheelchair.

Finally, he jumped out of a plane over Mount Everest in a wingsuit (you know, those things that make people look like they're flying squirrels) and flew all the way down to the base of the mountain, where he landed gracefully—in his wheelchair.

People all over the world watched Ethan's videos. They clapped and cheered and sent him emails asking how he did it. People made T-shirts and asked for his autograph. The whole time, Ethan was in his head, wondering if he'd made the right choice. After all, being a daredevil stuntman was cool, but playing basketball was even cooler.

"I guess you proved me wrong," Lucy said. "Good job. Looks like we're going to be in business together for a long time. What do you want to do next?"

"Continue proving you wrong," Ethan said. "Let's go play basketball."

CHAPTER 13
Classroom 13

For some odd reason, Lucy LaRoux, famous agent of Ace Agent Agency, didn't even consider representing Classroom 13. The 13th Classroom tried to speak up and say it wanted to be famous, but the students (as usual) were being far too loud.

Filled with jealousy and rage, the 13th Classroom vowed revenge (for the third time) on all of Ms. Linda's students and also that terrible Lucy LaRoux....

CHAPTER 14
Ximena

As Lucy looked for her next ~~victim~~ client, she found Ximena sitting at her desk quietly sketching flowers.

"What do you want to be famous for?" Lucy asked. "What's your talent?"

"I don't have any talent," Ximena said. (Which was a silly thing to say, as every child is good at something, whether they know it or not.)

"Everyone has something that can be ~~exploited~~ used," Lucy said. "For instance, your art. Let me see those sketches...."

"I like to draw flowers," Ximena said as Lucy flipped through her sketchbook. Each and every page was covered in sketches of flowers.

"I've seen enough," Lucy said. "You're coming to New York City with me. Time for the modern art world to meet their newest sensation: Ximena!"

Once Ximena got to New York City, Lucy put her up in a studio and told her to draw until she couldn't feel her hand. And that's exactly what Ximena did. She drew big flowers and small flowers. She sketched fat flowers and skinny flowers. She painted bright flowers and dark flowers.

After only a week, she'd made thousands of pictures of flowers. Lucy LaRoux framed them and put them up in a gallery. They were going to have the biggest art opening ever....

Ahem. Can I interrupt the story for a second? Believe it or not, your ol' pal Honest Lee here has been to a few art openings and knows a thing or two about the snooty art world. Let me explain how it works for you:

There is *free* cheese at art openings. Eat as much as you want. There's always more. Don't let them tell you otherwise. Even if they say, "Honest Lee, leave some for the other patrons!" Eat all you want. Cheese is awesome—unless of course you're lactose intolerant.

It was Ximena's big night, so she wore her favorite flower dress, which her *abuela* had made for her. She only expected maybe twenty people to show up for her show. Instead, hundreds came! There was a line out the door of people trying to get in. The art world loved her flowers. And, more important, they loved Ximena.

"She's so nice," they said.

"And easy to talk to," others said.

"And her art? The flowers are more real than...real flowers!"

Millionaires paid millions for her artistic renderings of flowers. "I can't even tell what kind of flower this is," one rich man said, "which means it's obviously the best and I need to buy it at any cost."

"Sold!" Lucy shouted, counting the piles of cash.

Yes, art types and critics alike loved Ximena's portraits of flowers. She was the newest artist of her age, and the best part was, this was only the beginning.

The next day, Lucy said, "Okay, things in the art world are always moving and changing, so what are you going to draw next?"

"More flowers, I guess," Ximena said. "That's all I know how to draw."

"Surely you can do more than just flowers," Lucy said. "Try to draw a person. Or a puppy. Or some stars!" Ximena drew a person, a puppy, and some stars. But they all looked like flowers.

"Try a robot, or a cowboy, or some skulls!" Lucy said. Ximena drew a robot, a cowboy, and some skulls. They all looked like flowers, too.

"Try a house, or an ocean, or some saltine crackers!" Ximena drew a house, an ocean, and some saltine crackers. They, too, all looked like flowers.

"I give up," Lucy said.

"Oh, I can do kittens!" Ximena said.

"Yes, do that!"

Ximena drew a kitten, but it looked like a flower, too.

"If you can't draw anything else, your art career is over," Lucy said. Ximena shrugged. She didn't mind. She really liked drawing flowers.

CHAPTER 15
Hugo

Bien qu'Hugo était français, il avait toujours adoré la musique country américaine. Cette musique parlait de courage, de grand amour et aussi de barbecue, qu'il adorait. Ses chanteurs préférés venaient du Texas, d'Alabama et de Géorgie. Et il pensait que les vieux westerns étaient les meilleurs films.

Alors, lorsqu'il a pu essayer de devenir célèbre, il a tout de suite su ce qu'il voulait être : un chanteur de country! Hugo jouait de la guitare et écrivait des chansons depuis qu'il avait cinq ans. Cela impressionna Lucy, qui le mit sur la scène du Grand Ole Opry à Nashville dans le Tennessee. Malheureusement, comme toutes les chansons d'Hugo étaient en français, personne ne pouvait comprendre le moindre mot de ce qu'il chantait.

CHAPTER 16
Ava

"**A**nd what are *you* good at?" Lucy asked Ava.

"Well, I'm a really good friend, and I like animals, and I play tennis really good—" Ava started.

"*Well,*" Ms. Linda corrected. "You don't play *good,* you play *well.*"

"Right," Ava said. "I play *well. Weller* than most. I'm the *wellest* at tennis."

"That's *not* grammatically correct," Ms. Linda said.

"Who cares about grammar?" Lucy said. "Can't you see this kid is going to be a famous tennis player?!"

The next thing Ava knew, she was playing at the Australian Open in Melbourne. It turns out Ava really was the *wellest* at tennis. She beat everyone in the outback—even a kangaroo.

She was exhausted. (She hated naps, but for the first time in her life, she really wanted nothing more than to take one.)

After that, Ava flew to the French Open in Paris. She'd never been to Paris before, and she couldn't wait to see the Louvre museum. She played game after game—and won each time. "Can I go see the Louvre now?" Ava asked after she won first place.

"Not right now," Lucy said. "You need to keep playing tennis if you want to be famous for it."

Ava flew to the US Open in New York City. Ava's uncles lived there, and the rest of the family came to see her. Everyone was excited to have a family reunion. "You can see them after you win," Lucy said. So Ava played and played and played. Once again, she won first place.

But Lucy had a plane waiting for her. "You'll have to see your family next time. You got an invitation to play in the Wimbledon Championships in London. You can't say no!"

Ava felt terrible. "I miss my family and I'm tired of playing tennis."

"Do you want to be known as the world's *wellest* tennis player?" Lucy asked.

"Yeah, I think so," Ava answered, now unsure.

"Then you have to keep playing."

Ava flew to London. There, she beat every famous tennis player, male and female, in the whole world. But before they gave her the title of the *Wellest Tennis Player in the Whole World*, one more person wanted to play her—the queen of England!

"I can't beat the queen in tennis!" Ava said, thinking of her own lovely grandmother Shirley. "That would be rude!"

"Don't you want to be famous?!" Lucy shouted.

Ava thought about it. She really did like tennis, but maybe it wasn't worth embarrassing the queen of England. Plus, she missed her family, especially her cousins—Angelina, Siena, Sophia, Taylor, and Morgan. Ava was surprised to find she even missed her brother.

"I'm done with fame," Ava said. She handed her tennis racket to Lucy and went home.

CHAPTER 17
William

Lucy LaRoux was a Hollywood agent. That meant she usually judged people based purely on looks. So when she saw William Wilhelm, she said, "Puny, short, wears glasses...you must be the class genius!"

"What? Who? Me?" William said. "Nope!"

"Yeah, we'll get you on some game shows!" Lucy said, ignoring him. "You'll solve math problems, or answer trivia questions, or spell big words no one's ever heard of, or... What's wrong? You look confused. I thought that didn't happen to smart people."

"That's because I'm not the smartest kid in class," William explained.

"That'd be me." Mason waved. "F-a-r-t, that spells 'smart'!"

"It does not," Olivia said. "Actually, I'm the smart one in this class. Possibly the only one." Olivia went back to doing long division—for fun.

"So what do you want to be famous for?" Lucy asked William.

"I want to be a famous rapper," William said.

Now it was Lucy who looked confused. She shrugged. "Okay, MC Willy, show me what you got."

William picked up a pencil, pretending it was a mic. He turned his hat sideways and did his rap:

"Yo, yo, yo!

♫

My name is Willy,

and I'd like to say,

"I am a student in school,   ♫

in the Classroom THIRTEEN!

"Boom!" ~~MC Willy~~ William said. He dropped his pretend mic to the floor. No one applauded.

"You do realize raps are supposed to *rhyme*, right?" Lucy said.

Confused, William scratched his head. "They are?"

CHAPTER 18
Emma

When it was Emma's turn, something very strange happened. Lucy couldn't find her talent contracts, or her pen, or her purse. They had all vanished into thin air.

"I've been robbed!" Lucy screamed.

But as Lucy was about to have a panic attack, Emma revealed each of the missing items—by pulling them out of a top hat.

"Ta-da!" Emma said with a smile.

The room burst into applause.

"Bravo!" Mason shouted. "B-a-r-f, that spells 'bravo'!"

"No it doesn't." Olivia rolled her eyes.

Emma put the top hat on and took a small bow for Lucy. "I want to be a famous magician. I already know five good tricks, my assistant works for free, and I'm okay to travel coach to save on expenses."

And that's how the *Emm*-azing Emma was born. The Ace Agent Agency booked her at birthday parties and small theaters to see how well she'd perform. Emma nailed every show, wowing the audience with her five unbelievable illusions:

Trick 1: Emma could pull animals out of her hat. First, a rabbit. Then a bald eagle. And finally a lion. "Abracadabra!"

Trick 2: Emma could change stuffed animals into real animals. First, a bear. Then a giraffe. And finally a tiger. "Alakazam!"

Trick 3: Emma could blow bubbles through her fingers. Then she could make them into balloon animals. They were usually cats. "Sim-sala-bim-cat!"

Trick 4: Emma could remove her own head and bounce it on her arms. This usually made someone in the crowd faint. "Shazam!"

Trick 5: Emma could use her wand to make someone in the audience levitate—which means to rise or hover in the air. "Hocus-pocus!"

The *Emm*-azing Emma's popularity grew fast. Before she knew it, she was performing a SOLD-OUT show in Madison Square Garden. But before her show, a group of six strange adults walked into her dressing room.

"Who are you?" Emma asked.

"We are the secretive Magicka Society, a community of professional illusionists," said the short, squat man in a purple cape.

"We have seen your shows and would like you to join us," said a tall, thin woman who wore a red velvet cape.

"All you need to do is to tell us *how* you do your magic," said a rather large man wearing a cape of gold sequins.

"I'd love to join," Emma said. "I don't mind sharing, but there's nothing to share. It's just magic."

The Magicka Society didn't believe her. "Are you using mirrors to trick our eyes so that it looks like your head is off your shoulders?" one magician asked.

"It's a hologram! You're using computer and camera equipment! I saw a news story about this. With my mom. Who I still live with!" said another.

"No, no, no, you fools! It's a puppet! She uses a series of pulleys and strings to create her illusions!" said a third magician.

"Nope, nope, nope," Emma said. "It's just magic. Here, I can prove it!"

With a wave of her hand, the *Emm*-azing

Emma *poofe*d into a cloud of smoke, then reappeared on top of the large magician with a funny mustache. She took off her head and handed it to him.

"See? No mirrors, no computers, no strings," Emma's head said.

The society members freaked out, tossing her head from one to the other. Emma finally caught her head and put it back on.

"No fair!" the mustached magician said. "You're using *real* magic! You're a...a...a... WITCH!"

With torches, the six strange adults chased Emma onto the stage. "She's a witch! A witch!" they shouted to the crowd.

"Boo!" the crowd hissed. Apparently, people like fake magic. Not real magic. The *Emm*-azing Emma's professional magic career was over.

A single tear ran down Emma's cheek. Then she hopped on a broom with her rabbit and flew away.

CHAPTER 19
Liam

Lucy sniffed something and felt sick. She held her nose and waved away a fart cloud. "Did you do that?" Lucy asked.

"Guilty as charged," Liam said, tipping his Viking helmet to her. Liam stood there with a devilish grin and a milk mustache above his lip.

"I'll work with you, but you can't fart around me," Lucy said. "Understood?"

"Works for me. I may be able to fart the national anthem, but I don't want to be famous for farts. I've broken records, I've come back from the dead, and I used to breathe underwater. Everybody thinks they know what I'm going to do next, but I'm ready to shock them. Let's aim higher, like two hundred stories higher."

"Where are you going with this?" Lucy asked, already bored.

"Straight to the top of the world's tallest diving board, woman! And I'm taking the whole world with me!"

The stunt made national news. They showed images of a diving board two hundred stories in the air. On the ground was a swimming pool full of chocolate pudding. News reporters hovered, talking to their viewers like they were about to witness the greatest event in the history of humankind.

"In just a few short minutes, local legend Liam Lancaster, a young man who refuses to remove his Viking helmet, will attempt the impossible! A two-hundred-story belly flop into a pool of chocolate pudding! Will he survive?!"

"Absolutely," Liam said, starting his climb up the ladder. The first twenty stories were easy enough. He turned and flexed for the cameras, then waved to family and friends.

But by the time Liam reached fifty stories up, he began to feel nauseous. Maybe eating all those corn dogs right before wasn't the best idea. Liam tried to shake it off and kept climbing.

One thousand feet...one thousand five hundred feet...two thousand feet...the people looked like ants...and then smaller than ants...and then he couldn't see them.

As someone who rode roller coasters every chance he got, Liam never thought he'd be afraid of heights. But now the air was thinning at this height. The worst part was his hands wouldn't stop sweating. He had to be careful climbing the ladder.

When Liam finally reached the diving board, he clung to the rail. Then he looked down. Big mistake. The world was so far away. His knees knocked together. From the ground, people looked up with binoculars. It looked like Liam was doing a funny dance on purpose, but he wasn't. Liam was afraid.

Liam looked over the edge of the diving board. If he misjudged the angle of the belly flop, he'd be a pancake, and not the tasty kind. "I regret this decision!" he shouted to the wind.

Liam couldn't do it. It was just too…terrifying. He turned around to climb back down the ladder, just as a strong gust of wind blew his Viking helmet off his head! When he reached for it, he slipped.

Liam was now free-falling two hundred stories straight down!

As he fell, his life flashed before his eyes: It was just a series of wonderful, hilarious farts. Maybe he should go back to farts....

The ground got closer and closer...two thousand feet...one thousand five hundred feet...one thousand feet...five hundred feet...

Liam said his prayers. That's when the *Emm*-azing Emma—Classroom 13's only witch—flew straight toward him on her broom. Just as Liam was about to crash into the ground, Emma swooped in and caught Liam (and his Viking helmet). As they landed safely on the ground, Liam fainted—then farted.

"Gross," Emma said.

As his eyes slowly opened, Liam whispered, "That was fart for 'thank you.'"

CHAPTER 20
Fatima

"Are you an actress?" Lucy asked Fatima.

"Who, me?" Fatima said. "No."

"That's a shame because I told my movie studio friends I had an actress, but things didn't really work out with *him*."

"But they let me keep this!" Mason said, climbing back into the cardboard box like a kitten.

"Are you sure you're not an actress, kiddo?"

Fatima blushed. "No—but I'm really good at reading comics."

"Any interest in starring in a comic book movie?!" Lucy asked. "Those are all the rage right now!"

"*Comic book movie?!*" Fatima said, unable to hide her smile. She considered the possibilities....

No more cosplay with cheap costumes—she could wear a movie-grade supersuit. On-screen, she'd be a real superhero, blasting special-effects lasers out of her eyes or maybe even flying. She could be on panels with her favorite comic book movie characters. And best of all, she'd be the first to see her comic book movie—before anyone else!

"Ever heard of the *Super Squad?*" Lucy asked as she scanned emails on her phone. "They're looking for new cast members for the sequel."

"*Super Squad?!* It's only my favorite comic book movie of all time!" Fatima squealed with delight. "Count me in!!"

Amazingly, Fatima was cast in the sequel to her favorite movie. Not so amazingly, Fatima was *not* cast as a super*hero*—she was cast as a super*villain*.

She would be the evil Porcupina, the half-human, half-porcupine nemesis with spikes all over her body. This was terrible. Fatima hated Porcupina. So did most comic book fans. Porcupina sliced and diced their favorite heroes, and almost destroyed them on multiple occasions. She was cruel, awful, and just plain mean. She was the most sinister and deadly villain the *Super Squad* had ever faced in the comic books.

But this was Fatima's chance to meet the cast and be part of a superhero franchise. She couldn't pass it up. So she stayed her course and played the villainess. After filming had wrapped, Fatima and the rest of the actors from *Super Squad* were invited to San Diego Comic-Con.

As Fatima walked out on stage, the announcer said, "Introducing the bad girl you love to hate: Porcupina!"

But rather than clapping and cheering, the fans went crazy with rage. They booed and hissed, tossing half-eaten corn dogs at her. One fan even threw a Porcupina action figure. Its tiny plastic spikes really hurt!

Fatima was sad. No one at Comic-Con wanted a picture with her. Her costars were scared to be seen with her. She smelled like corn dogs. And worst of all, a mob of angry fans chased her out of the auditorium, shouting, "Stay away from our heroes, evildoer!"

"It's just a movie!" Fatima yelled. That only made the fans even more mad.

Fatima declined to go to the red carpet

premiere. Instead, she stayed home and watched the first *Super Squad* movie—alone.

Don't feel too bad for Fatima—she made a million dollars from the movie.

Then again, famous agent Lucy LaRoux took most of that.

CHAPTER 21
Mark

Everyone knew Mark was the most handsome boy in class. So when Lucy came to his desk, she immediately said, "Let's make you a model."

"Actually," Mark said, "I've always wanted to be a comedian."

"But you're so gorgeous," Lucy argued. "You're the universal idea of what beautiful looks like. I can make you the poster boy for just about anything."

"Yeah, but I don't want to be known for my good looks. I want people to know what's *inside*. That's what counts, right?"

Lucy started laughing. She kept laughing.

"What's so funny?" Mark asked.

"You *are* funny!" Lucy said. "But honestly, no one in Hollywood cares what's in your heart or your head—not unless you're a writer. Like Honest Lee. I represent him. And everyone likes his writing. Don't they?"

Mark and Lucy both looked right off this page and looked at *you*. What do you think of the writing?

CHAPTER 22
Zoey

Mark didn't want to be a model, but Zoey sure did. "Not just any model—I want to be a *super-model!*" Zoey said.

Lucy shook her head. "I'm sorry, gorgeous, but you're too short. Supermodels are tall." It was true. Supermodels are usually very tall, and Zoey was the shortest girl in Classroom 13.

"But it's my dream!" Zoey said.

"I once had a dream," Lucy said. "And life crushed it. That's why I became an agent. Do you want to be an agent? You could rep models."

Zoey thought of helping other people to become models while she remained a...*non*-model. The thought was too much for Zoey, and she began to cry. She buried her face in her hands—her soft, well-shaped, perfectly sized, beautiful hands.

"Those hands!" Lucy said. "They're stunning!" She took off her watch and handed it to Zoey. "Put this on!" Lucy told her, forcing the watch around Zoey's wrist.

Lucy gasped with awe. The watch had never looked better. It was a real-life vision that could be on a billboard over Sunset Boulevard. Zoey's hands were perfect for modeling rings, bracelets, gloves, and more.

"Kid, I take it all back. You *are* going to be a supermodel," Lucy said.

Zoey leapt up with excitement. "I am?!"

"Yes! A HAND model!"

Zoey was usually very picky and particular, but in this case, she didn't care. As her class-mates cheered for her, Liam went in to high-five Zoey, but Lucy stopped him.

"Nuh-uh, Mister! Those hands are *never* to be touched. They are now Ace Agent Agency property." (So Liam high-fived himself.)

Lucy immediately took Zoey to get fitted for protective gloves. The pair of gloves were made of titanium metal on the outside and the soft-est silk on the inside. "These will keep your pre-cious hands safe when you're not working," Lucy explained.

The following day, Zoey began her hand-modeling career. She modeled the newest watches, the most expensive rings, the craziest nail art, and a variety of lotions and hand soaps.

Zoey's hands became famous! Well, at least

on commercials. But her hands were working so much, Zoey never got a break. She liked being a model, but she did not like working. She was tired, and her hands were exhausted.

That night, when she got home, she went to put on her protective gloves. But they didn't fit. Zoey tried and tried to shove her fingers in there, but somehow, her hands were too big.

"I think my gloves shrank," Zoey told Lucy.

Lucy shrieked. "Your hands! Your glorious hands! What happened to them?! They're... they're *huge*!"

"They look the same, though," Zoey said.

"It doesn't matter. Little-girl hands sell products. Man hands don't."

Lucy tried to hide the problem. But on set, Zoey's hands were too big for the jewelry. The photographer took one look and said, "You can't model our dainty product with those meat hooks. You're fired. Sorry, not sorry."

"But, please, I can still model!" Zoey pleaded, trying to grab the photographer. Her hands were so strong that she crushed his camera without meaning to.

"I can fix it! I can still do this!" Zoey said.

"Talk to the hand," the photographer said, holding up his normal-sized hand, which was smaller than Zoey's. "Get off my set."

Lucy was about destroy Zoey's contract when she got a call. "Looks like I need a man-hands model. How do you feel about modeling boxing gloves, men's deodorant, and paper towels?" Lucy asked.

"Do I still get to be called a supermodel?" Zoey asked.

"Sure." Lucy shrugged. And that's how Zoey started her modeling career.

CHAPTER 23
Teo

"**L**et's get me famous," Teo said to Lucy as soon as it was his turn.

"And what's your talent?" Lucy asked.

Teo pulled out his phone and showed her his homepage. "I want to be a world-famous YouTube star," Teo said. "I have forty-seven followers, but I can do better. I have ideas. Lots of ideas."

"I like you, kid." Lucy smiled. "Let's get started."

Lucy followed Teo around for days and days and days. She recorded everything and uploaded it to social media. Then she had her other famous clients post and repost, again and again. In a matter of days, Teo had *forty-seven million* followers.

"Much better!" Lucy said. "But now we need to build your brand."

"My brand?" Teo said, confused. "But I'm already famous. I have forty-seven million followers."

"That's nothing! If you want to stay famous, you have to keep up the hard work," Lucy explained. "You need a *brand*. What makes you *you?*"

"Um, well, I like video games and movies and goofing around...."

"Perfect! That's your brand!" Lucy said.

So Lucy and the Ace Agent Agency camera crew followed Teo around. They filmed him playing video games, talking about his favorite movies, and goofing around on his skateboard.

But as Sunday rolled around, he remembered he had plans.

"Sorry, I can't film today," Teo said. "I have plans with my grandpa Walt. We're going kayaking and then mountain biking."

"Kayaking and mountain biking are *IN*," Lucy said. "But grandfathers are *OUT*. No one wants to see grandparents doing fun things."

"I do," Teo said.

"Do you want to be famous, or don't you?" Lucy asked.

Teo thought about it. "I really do like being a famous Internet star, but…well, famous is temporary, but family is forever."

As Teo walked away from his fame, he felt good about himself. When he went home, he and his grandfather made the funniest, most famous Internet video ever. It turned out Lucy was wrong about grandparents being *OUT*. They are very much *IN*.

CHAPTER 24
Chloe

"**R**eady to be famous and rich?" Lucy asked Chloe.

"Famous, yes," Chloe answered. "Rich, no."

Lucy didn't understand. But that's because she didn't understand Chloe.

Chloe cared deeply—about everything. She never met a can she didn't want to donate, or a tree she didn't want to plant, or a paper she

didn't want to recycle. Chloe loved her causes. Why? Because...

Chloe *cared*.

"I want to make the world a better place," Chloe explained to Lucy.

"I don't get you, kid," Lucy said.

"I have an idea. It's a nonprofit charity called the Care-plane Society," Chloe said. "Like *airplane*, only it's *Care*-plane, because we care—"

"Yeah, I got it," Lucy snipped.

"So what we do is the Ace Agent Agency buys an airplane, and I'll fill it with food and medicine and school supplies. Then we fly the plane all over the world, dropping off goods to those in need. We would put it up on social media and get people to donate food and medicine and school supplies. Or they can just donate money—"

That got Lucy's attention.

"I like money!" Lucy squealed. "Hmmm. I suppose this would be a huge tax break for the Ace Agent Agency. My boss will like that. Genius!"

"That's not what I meant," Chloe whispered. But she went along with it so that she could make the Care-plane idea into a real thing. People in need would have food and medicine and school supplies, and that's what really counted.

Chloe organized everything. There were places to drop off food, hospitals that would donate medicine, and large companies to provide free school supplies. But Chloe needed someone to run the website for money donations. She looked online and found a successful New York businessman to organize the donations. His name was Jeremiah Jerk.

"It's pronounced *Jerr*," he explained. "The *k* is silent."

Then Chloe and Lucy put together a huge celebrity bash to raise awareness about the Care-plane Society. Together, they raised millions and millions of dollars. Chloe couldn't believe it. Her dream to help others was about to come true.

Only it wasn't.

It turns out Jeremiah *Jerr* really was Jeremiah *Jerk*, famous con man. He wasn't putting the money in the Care-plane Society's account. He was putting it into his own pockets. He stole the money, then stole the actual Care-plane. He flew it out of the country and didn't drop a single dollar, canned good, medicine, or school supply on anyone's head—rich or poor.

He was never heard from again.

The Care-plane Society was now penniless, planeless, and helpless. And Chloe—poor Chloe who cared so much—was known, *infamously*, as a thief.

CHAPTER 25
Earl

When Lucy came to Earl, she took one look at the class hamster and said, "Ew. It stinks. No celebrity potential there. I'm *not* going anywhere near that rodent."

Rodent?! Earl thought. He was *very* offended. He'd show that awful agent a thing or two....

CHAPTER 26
Mya & Madison

"**W**e want our own clothing line, our own perfume, and our own TV show," Madison & Mya explained to Lucy. No one in Classroom 13 wanted fame more than the twins.

"But what's your talent?"

"We don't have any," the twins said. (Remember what I said in Ximena's chapter, about every child having a talent? I meant that. But in this case, Mya & Madison were right. They didn't have any talents.)

"No talent?" Lucy smiled. "Then you're perfect for *reality TV*."

After school, Mya & Madison went home to find their house had been taken over by a TV crew. Camera guys and sound teams and makeup assistants wandered in and out of every room. There were even a bunch of writers.

"What do we need writers for?" the twins asked. "Isn't reality TV supposed to be based on reality?"

The writers all laughed. "In reality TV, *real* moments are all totally fake, scripted stuff we think up when we're on the toilet."

"Oh," Mya & Madison said, confused. They sat down at their desks to do their homework, like usual.

But the director stopped them and asked, "What are you doing?"

"Our homework."

"Nope. That's boring. This is reality TV. You need to spice it up," the director said. "People want to watch people fighting! Let's have the two of you fight over this pencil. And...roll the cameras. ACTION!"

The girls stood there, confused.

"But why would we fight over a pencil?" Mya said.

"We have more pencils in the drawer," said Madison.

"Pretend you don't!" the director growled.

"ACTIOOOON!" the director shouted again. "Roll the cameras. ACTION!"

The girls pretended to fight. Mya pretended to yell at Madison, and Madison pretended to keep the pencil away from her sister. But after a while, the twins forgot they were acting and started fighting for real. They screamed and pushed each other and pulled each other's hair. They even knocked over a table with their mom's favorite lamp. It broke into a thousand pieces.

"Perfect! I love it! Give me more!" the director called out.

So Mya & Madison gave him more—more fights, more arguments, and more tantrums. The girls were getting good at being mean to each other. But the moment the cameras turned off, they apologized and went back to loving each other.

Their reality show, *Mya & Madison: TWINning at Life!* was a huge success. The girls had their show, they had a new clothing line, and a new fragrance. The twin sisters felt like they had finally made it—

—until the gossip blogs online started making up stories about them. Some of the headlines included:

MADISON KILLS ALLIGATOR, MAKES IT INTO PURSE!

MYA HIRES ORPHANS TO CLEAN BATHROOM FLOORS!

REALITY TV TWINS POUR OIL ON PENGUINS, ON PURPOSE!

MYA & MADISON, NOT REAL TWINS!

Of course, none of that was true. (Well, Mya *did* hire some orphans to scrub her bathroom tub, but only because her mom insisted they still do their chores at home.) But it still hurt the girls that people *really* thought that about them.

When Mya & Madison felt like they couldn't take it anymore, Lucy taught them the harsh truth about reality TV: The negative press was part of why the show worked. Some fans hated to love them, and others loved to hate them. But the most important thing was that the people kept watching their show, no matter what.

Mya & Madison agreed. Being infamous wasn't so bad. So they kept fake-fighting for the cameras. It turns out they did have a hidden talent after all.

CHAPTER 27

Jacob

One kid in Classroom 13 knew TV better than he knew the freckles on the back of his hand. (Oddly enough, one of those freckles was shaped like a TV.) That kid was Jacob Jones.

Lucy sat on his desk and said, "I like your face. You should be on TV."

"I don't know," Jacob said. "I've had a taste of celebrity life, and it wasn't as great as I'd hoped.

You can't go anywhere without people recognizing and harassing you. It's kind of awful."

"What if you could be famous *without* people seeing your face?" Lucy asked with a sly smile.

"I'm listening. . . ." Jacob said, intrigued.

"By any chance, do you like Mario's Meatballs & Spaghetti?"

"The ones that come in a can? I love it! I eat it for dinner all the time!" Jacob said.

And so Lucy cast Jacob in a commercial—but not as himself. He wore a costume that transformed him into a mascot for his favorite canned spaghetti. As Meatball Mario, Jacob became a singing, dancing stack of meatballs covered in spaghetti. His character would dance under a shower of Parmesan cheese and sing songs to entice kids to eat his canned goods. At the end of each commercial, fireworks would explode all around him as he said his tagline:

"Mario's Meatballs are magically mouthwatering!"

Jacob loved the idea. He got to be on TV during his favorite shows, but he didn't have to put up with any fans chasing him around town.

But after a few hours of actual work, Jacob could barely breathe. It was so hot inside the suit, he would sweat like a man crossing the Sahara without water. All that sweating made his face break out in pimples. And it made him stink, too. After filming, he didn't want to be seen—or smelled—in public. And when the fireworks went off, he almost always got burned.

Needless to say, Jacob wasn't happy.

"I can't keep doing this," Jacob told Lucy. "I've lost twenty pounds, I stink every day, and my face looks like a pizza."

"Do you want to do pizza commercials, too?" Lucy asked.

"No!" Jacob said. "I don't want this job anymore. It's not as fun as I thought it would be."

"Sorry, kid," Lucy said. "You signed a life-time contract to appear in Meatball Mario

CHAPTER 28
Olivia

As the resident know-it-all of Classroom 13, Olivia Ogilvy had a lot of thoughts about things. She had thoughts about Ms. Linda, opinions about her classmates, and even a theory that the 13th Classroom was alive...which is ridiculous. (Isn't it?)

To earn her fame, Olivia wrote all her thoughts down. It became a series of very popular books.

You may have heard of them. She wrote her books under a *pen name*. A pen name is a fake name that writers sometimes use to hide their true identity.

What's that? Did she write *this* series? *Um*... I don't know!

CHAPTER 29
Lily

Famous agent Lucy LaRoux's cell phone rang. She took one look at the caller ID and turned pale. "It's my boss." She gulped. She answered, "Hello?"

Judging by all the screaming coming from the phone, it did *not* sound like good news for her. In between bursts of shouting, the kids in Classroom 13 heard Lucy whisper:

"Yep...Uh-huh...I'm *so, so* sorry....I know, you're right....But it wasn't my fault....It will never happen again....I'm begging you....Okay, got it...Thank you...I won't let you down!"

Lucy turned off her phone and glared at the students of Classroom 13. "Is everything okay?" Ms. Linda asked her cousin.

"No, everything is *not* okay," Lucy said. "Right now, about half of your students have made me money, and the other half has cost me money. My boss is not happy. But we have one chance to make things right...."

Then Lucy got down on her knees in front of Lily. "You're the last student left. Please, please, *please* tell me that you're going to help me get a win for the Ace Agent Agency."

"Well, I want to be an astronaut, but I'm still too young. However, I do have all kinds of science-y ideas for inventions. For the last month, I've been building one to prank my four brothers...." Lily pulled the small device from her backpack. It looked like a little metal egg. "I call it the LILY-HAMMER 5000."

"What is it?" Lucy asked.

"It's an EMP," Lily answered.

The agent scratched her head. "Does that stand for: Egg Making Power?"

"No, it stands for Electromagnetic Pulse," Lily explained. "The Lily-Hammer 5000 emits an invisible pulse of EM energy that knocks out all electronics in a one-room radius. It makes TVs turn off, computers go to sleep, and phones shut down. But not forever. Everything will power back on again after an hour. I don't wanna break people's stuff; I just want to *prank* people.

"I've been doing it to my brothers all week. Every time they play their video games, I shut them down right before they beat a level. They have no idea it's me. It drives them nuts!"

"That's so cool!" said Yuna and Ava.

"That's so cruel!" said Dev and Teo.

"It looks like an egg, though," Lucy said. "Can it prank people *and* make eggs?"

"No," Lily said.

Lucy considered the egg-shaped machine. Even though she didn't quite understand it, Lucy did know that people liked technology and gizmos. "Okay, if that's the best you've got, let's see what I can do with it."

Lucy sent Lily's blueprints to the Ace Agent Agency. They filed a patent and started production immediately.

Pre-orders for the Lily-Hammer 5000® were in the millions. Pranksters of all ages couldn't wait to mess with their friends and families. The prank device cost three hundred bucks each, but no one cared. They wanted it.

The Ace Agent Agency was pleased with the sales numbers, and Lucy's boss told her she "did good." Things were looking up for Lucy and the Ace Agent Agency.

On the day it came out, Lily tried to turn on her computer. She wanted to read the reviews and the blogs and see what people thought of something she'd made. But her computer wouldn't turn on.

In fact, neither would her phone. Or her tablet. Or her TV.

Nothing worked.

That was because everyone in the country who bought a Lily-Hammer 5000 got their package shipped to them in the mail at the exact same time. That meant everyone in the country opened the package at the exact same time. That also meant everyone in the country turned on their own personal Lily-Hammer 5000 at the exact same time...

...and that created one giant EMP so massive it fried nearly every device in the country. No one could call or text or play silly games on their phones.

Everyone *freaked* out. Society went crazy. Many

believed it was a return to the technological dark ages. Needless to say, people were furious.

Lucy was so mad her face was the color of…well, I can't think of a metaphor, so let's just say her face was really, really *red*. "I thought you said the pranked phones would turn back on after an hour?" Lucy yelled.

"They were supposed to…." Lily said, rechecking her notes and calculations. "Oh, I see what happened. People weren't supposed to use their Lily-Hammers at the same time. We should have put a warning on the box."

"Now you tell me!" Lucy shouted. "I told you this thing should've made eggs!"

Technology in the country did not turn back on after an hour. Or twelve hours. Or twenty-four hours.

The Ace Agent Agency started getting letters—

actual letters, in the mail, with stamps. The letters were all complaints.

"How am I supposed to order a pizza without my cell phone?" one angry letter said. "I am starving!"

"How am I supposed to text my friend Jeff 'you are kewl' with a sunglasses emoji?" another angry letter said. "Now Jeff probably thinks I'm mad at him!"

"What am I supposed to do in the bathroom? Just use the bathroom?! I like to play games on the toilet! This is madness!" said a third letter (probably written while on the toilet).

Finally, the president declared a state of national emergency and demanded that people destroy their Lily-Hammer 5000s. To help people calm down, the president also bought everyone a new phone. After all, *she* was a very good president. (Yes, the president in this world is a woman, and she is a very good president at that!)

Then Madam President demanded the Ace Agent Agency refund everyone's money. Immediately.

Lily may have been embarrassed that her invention broke the country. But her embarrassment was nothing compared to the rage Lucy LaRoux was feeling at this moment. Lucy was in big trouble at her job, and Lucy needed to blame someone....

CHAPTER 30
Infamous Lucy!

On Friday, something occurred to Ms. Linda. "With all of you becoming famous and infamous, I honestly can't remember the last time we did any actual classwork," she said. "So... POP QUIZ!"

The students of Classroom 13 groaned. Some of the students were still famous (or *infamous*), but all of them still had to go to school. They prepared themselves for a boring, terrible, regular day of work, when—

—the door swung open, and a furious Lucy stormed in.

"*Stop whatever it is you're doing!*" Lucy shouted at them.

"Excuse me, Lucy LaRoux, but this is *my* classroom," Ms. Linda said. "You may be my cousin and a famous agent, but in here, I am in charge."

"No, no, no!" Lucy growled, stomping her feet on the floor and pitching a tantrum. "I have something to say, and all of you are going to listen!

"In all my time as a senior talent agent, I have *never* dealt with such horrible clients before! Look at all of you! Failed wrestlers and failed artists and failed actors—"

"I didn't fail. I quit," said Triple J.

"Same here," said Sophia.

"Me too," said Dev.

"When I say *fail*, I mean *failed to make me stinking rich!*" Lucy LaRoux screamed.

"Then you should have said so," Ms. Linda said. "After all, I don't think anyone in this class failed. I think everyone did a wonderful job."

"If they did such a wonderful job, then why is my job in jeopardy?!" Lucy asked.

"I suppose *our* goals and *your* goals were not in alignment—meaning, on the same path. If you feel the same way, perhaps you should nullify, or cancel, our contracts. Then all of us can go our separate ways, giving one another only well wishes," a voice said from the back of the class.

Everyone expected it to be Olivia (because of all the big words), but it turned out to be Mason.

Ms. Linda was impressed. She could hardly believe Mason—who believed Halloween candy was alive and could read his mind—formed such a structured and well-thought reply. It was *not* like Mason. "Mason, that was incredibly well spoken," she told him.

"Thank you," Mason said. "I hit my head this morning. My smarts will wear off soon. For now,

I'll return to my box." Mason climbed back into his empty box like a sleepy kitten.

"What is wrong with all of you?!" Lucy shouted. "You know what—it doesn't matter! You all work for me!"

She slammed their contracts down on Ms. Linda's desk. "None of you can just quit! I'll lose my job unless I make some real money off you kids, and that's just what we're going to do. You all signed these contracts, and contracts are *binding*, which means I *own* all of you! Kiss your families good-bye because you'll never see them again! You'll be too busy working for the rest of your lives! I don't care if you fulfill your contracts as celebrity toenail-clippers or circus pooper-scoopers or whatever other terrible jobs I can think of. You. Will. *WORK!*"

A hush fell over the class.

Some students started to cry. Others just got angry. They didn't like being famous *or* infamous. (And those who did like it really didn't like Lucy LaRoux—she had taken all their money and had yet to share the profits.)

"Now, listen here," Ms. Linda said. "You will *not* come into my classroom and bully these children. As far as I'm concerned, your contracts are already null and void."

With that, Ms. Linda took the stack of contracts and ripped them in half.

"YAAYYYY!" the students cheered. They'd never realized how awesome Ms. Linda was before now.

"Not so fast!" Lucy said with a sneaky sneer. "I have *copies*."

"BOOOOO!!" the students moaned.

But when Lucy opened her purse, she screamed. Earl crawled out with a fat belly and let out a long, rude *BURP*. He had gotten his revenge.

"That rodent ate my duplicates!" Lucy hissed.

"YAAYYYY!" the students cheered.

"No matter!" Lucy snapped. "I have *triplicates*!"

"BOOOOO!!" the students moaned.

But when Lucy opened her briefcase, the *Emm*-azing Emma snapped her fingers. The contracts *poof*ed into a cloud of purple smoke and glitter.

"Yay?" some of the students cheered. They weren't sure how many more copies Lucy LaRoux had.

And sure enough, Lucy smiled a wicked smile. "Good thing I have *digital* copies of the contracts on my phone! Hah!"

"Good thing I bought a Lily-Hammer," Ms. Linda said, grabbing something from her desk.

"Those are illegal!" Lucy said. "If you use one of those EMP Lily-Hammer things, you'll go to jail!"

"How silly of me. It's not a Lily-Hammer. It's just a regular hammer." Then Ms. Linda grabbed her cousin's phone and smashed it into a hundred little pieces.

Lucy's smile finally faded. All her copies were gone. There were no more contracts. The students of Classroom 13 were free once more.

Ms. Linda opened the door of Classroom 13 and pointed to the hallway. "I think it's time for you to go, Lucy LaRoux. We need to get back to learning."

Defeated, famous agent Lucy LaRoux scowled at the classroom and said, "You're all terrible, and you'll never be famous again!"

Little did Lucy know that the kids were already famous. This is the third book they've starred in. And they'll star in many more to come....

As they were no longer famous (or infamous), the students of Classroom 13 finished the school day like most students do—with some very *un*famous activities.

Instead of walking a red carpet, they walked the tiled classroom floor to turn in their homework.

Instead of signing autographs, they signed their names on quizzes and tests. And instead of smiling for cameras and journalists, they just smiled for their teacher, Ms. Linda, who had saved them from her terrible cousin.

Meanwhile, outside in the hall, famous agent Lucy LaRoux was kicking the 13th Classroom's door in anger. Like most living things, Classroom 13 did *not* like being kicked.

"*Stop it,*" whispered the classroom door.

Lucy looked around. "Who said that?"

"*I did,*" said the voice.

Lucy looked up and down the hallway, but there was no one around. Just her. And the door to Classroom 13.

"*Don't kick me again,*" the door said. "*It's rude.*"

Lucy figured this was some kind of prank. She roared, "I'll do what I want!"

Then she kicked the door again. This time, her leg went right through the door. Lucy tried to pull her leg back, but it was stuck in what felt like strawberry jelly. Then, like a strand of spaghetti, the door sucked her in completely. She was not in Classroom 13. She was somewhere...*else*.

"You should have made me famous," the 13th Classroom whispered. Then the door burped her out.

Lucy bounced into the hallway covered in slime. She had no idea what had happened or where she had been—but she was totally freaked. She ran out of the school, screaming and vowing to never work with children again.

Meanwhile, Ms. Linda and the students didn't hear a thing inside the 13th Classroom. They never did. But they would one day, one day rather soon....

CHAPTER 31
Your Chapter

That's right—it's your turn!

Grab some paper and a writing utensil. (Not a fork, silly. Try a pencil or pen.) Or if you have one of those fancy computer doo-hickeys, use that. Now tell me...

What do YOU want to be famous for?

When you're done, share it with your teacher, your family, and your friends. (Don't forget your pets! Pets like to hear stories, too.) You can even ask your parents to send me your chapter at the address below.

HONEST LEE

LITTLE, BROWN BOOKS FOR YOUNG READERS

1290 Avenue of the Americas

New York, NY 10104

Don't miss the next adventure with the students of Classroom 13!

When the 13th Classroom is struck by purple lightning, something strange happens—all the students get SUPERPOWERS!

You might think this is superb, but it is not. (It is sorta **SILLY**.) With great gifts come wild weather, atomic farts, spider-boy, and other **TRICKY** troubles. As the students of Classroom 13 are about to learn, getting superpowers is **NOT** always super.

HONEST LEE is a liar! You can't trust a thing he writes. He insists that his stories are true. And they're totally not! What's the truth? I have no idea. Honestly.

MATTHEW J. GILBERT is one of many Matthew Gilberts. Seriously. There's like a trillion of them. This particular Matthew Gilbert writes stories and has a nearly perfect mustache. When he's not writing about Classroom 13, he's watching monster movies, eating tacos, and singing made-up songs about his cats.

JOELLE DREIDEMY spent her childhood in the countryside among cows and books and has been drawing since she learned to walk. She lives in France, where she makes art for books, magazines, greeting cards, and more. When she's not illustrating, she sings and plays guitar in a rock band.

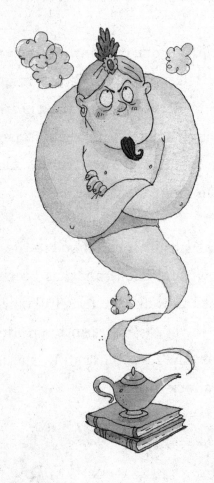